Island of the Nightingales

Prose Series 33

Canadä

Guernica Editions Inc. acknowledges the support of
The Canada Council for the Arts.
Guernica Editions Inc. acknowledges the support of
the Ontario Arts Council.
Guernica Editions Inc. acknowledges the financial support of the
Government of Canada through the Book Publishing Industry
Development Program (BPIDP).

CATERINA EDWARDS

ISLAND OF THE NIGHTINGALES

GUERNICA
TORONTO·BUFFALO·LANCASTER (U.K.)
2000

Copyright © 2000, by Caterina Edwards and Guernica Editions Inc.
All rights reserved. The use of any part of this publication, reproduced,
transmitted in any form or by any means, electronic, mechanical,
photocopying, recording or otherwise stored in a retrieval system, without
the prior consent of the publisher is an infringement of the copyright law.

Joseph Pivato, Guest Editor
Guernica Editions Inc.
P.O. Box 117, Station P, Toronto (ON), Canada M5S 2S6
2250 Military Road, Tonawanda, N.Y. 14150-6000 U.S.A.
Gazelle, Falcon House, Queen Square, Lancaster LA1 1RN U.K.

Some of these stories appeared in a different form in the following
publications: "Prima Vera" (*Alberta Bound*, NeWest Press, and *Ricordi*,
Guernica Editions); "Everlasting Life" (*Getting Here,* NeWest Press); "Home
and Away" *(Other Voices)*; "On a Platter (*Boundless Alberta,* NeWest Press);
"Multiculturalism" *(The Toronto Review of Contemporary Writing Abroad).*

Typeset by Selena.
Printed in Canada.
Legal Deposit – Fourth Quarter

National Library of Canada
Library of Congress Catalog Card Number: 00-107506
Canadian Cataloguing in Publication Data
Edwards, Caterina
Island of the nightingales
(Prose series ; 33)
ISBN 1-55071-022-2
I. Title. II Series.
PS8559.D83I84 2000   C813'.54   C00-901409-8
PR9199.3.E364I84 2000

Contents

Prima Vera / 7

Everlasting Life / 21

Island of the Nightingales / 44

Multiculturalism / 70

Home and Away / 89

On a Platter / 102

For Tatiania and Antonia and Marco always

Prima Vera

"The doctor," Cesare would say on his way out, "told me you must get more rest," picking up his lunch box and thermos, pulling on his gloves. "Go. Sleep," his last words before he wound his scarf around the bottom half of his face and turned to the door.

And Maria would obey him. That is, she would try. She would stretch out on their bed and close her eyes. Sleep, she would tell herself. Sleep. But then she would think of all the things Cesare had said the Doctor had said. *Toxemia, preclampsia*, Cesare had looked the words up in the Italian-English dictionary, but they weren't there. High-blood pressure. She understood that. She could feel the blood running through her veins, pushing too hard. Her heart beating too fast, too loud. She couldn't lie on her front; her stomach got too big. If she tried her side, she had to fiddle with the pillow. She was forced to lie on her back, her stomach protruding, forced to lie as if already laid out. And her hand, each time, strayed to her chest or throat. Her fingertips counting the beats. Runaway heart. And she couldn't get away. Runaway heart, and she was stuck to this miserable house, to this small drafty room, to the coming child, to the approaching day.

If she could be home in this time of waiting. If she could be with her sisters, her father. If she could see his faded blue eyes, feel his large knobbed hands on her hair, enter again his smell, lime and pipe tobacco. Home again. Then, she would not be afraid, then.

"How can you send me away – so far? How?"

And he had pulled away from her.

"He's your husband. Your place is with him."

Her place. What a place. Even in the panic of those last days before she had left her home to come and join Cesare, even then she had imagined it better than it was. So this is my America, she had thought when she first saw the house: the paint chipped and patchy, the front stairs cracked, the tiny front yard littered with old tires. "Mia casetta in Canada." None of the houses in her village were as flimsy as this one. Nor had she imagined how confined she would be to the house, locked in partly by her lack of English and her not being able to drive but mostly by the never-ending winter. A prisoner of this cold country. Month after month. Her very thoughts were freezing into the shape of the rooms and the furniture. And she could feel the fragile walls trying to hold off the snow, trying to keep back the cold. She could feel them buffeted, weakening.

The ice was pushing in at the windows, at the corners. Reaching for her.

How could she sleep? She hauled herself onto her side, feet on the floor, pushed up with a small grunt to a sitting position. She was enormous; the doctor was right about that. Though she had not liked his tone when he'd said, "Tell your wife not to eat so much spaghetti." She had told him, told him through Cesare, that she wasn't eating much. Couldn't. Three quarters of what went in came right back, from the first day onward, all eight months. But he had not paid attention. Just spoke louder "Less spaghetti." So she didn't tell him that they, *Veneti*, rarely ate the stuff.

The baby shifted, lurched. Maria, who had just got herself into a standing position, smoothed down her dress. That doctor could make all the accusations he wanted; she knew.

"It's feeding off me, sucking out my bones," she had said,

smiling at Cesare. "By the time it's born, there'll be nothing left of me." He had looked at her then, examined her face closely, trying to gauge the level of seriousness behind the light tone and light expression.

He had made a sound, a neutral sound. Then he fell back on his usual reassurance. "Everything will be fine. We're not in your village now. We have doctors – and a good hospital." But all evening his eyes had returned to her face. As if he suddenly wondered who this woman he'd chosen for a wife really was.

"So far and to a man I don't know."

"You will," her father had said, "you will know each other."

Cesare's old, open slippers slapped on the linoleum as Maria crossed the kitchen to the living room. She could no longer wear any of her own shoes. Her feet were swollen, doughy. Sometimes they were numb or prickly, and always she had to will them to move, pull them along. Her feet that used to run up the hill to her house, that used to fly, so it seemed, over the fields to her special spot, her circle of trees.

Maria sighed as she lowered herself carefully onto the battered sofa, then arranged her feet on the arm. Cesare was right. She was getting worse. Thinking things she shouldn't think. What had Beppi said? "Think beautiful thoughts. Concentrate on what is good and sweet and the baby will flourish."

Maria stared out the window at a bare tree, grey against the white snow and sky. She must think of spring. If she could concentrate hard enough. *Primavera*, she could call back that first truth. The scent of new grass, *prima*, the snowdrops at the base of her trees, *vera*, the buds on the branches, fresh and green and lacy.

She could see herself, hyacinths filling her arms, a hyacinth in her hair, buoyed by the sweet perfume. And beside her, in the gentle spring night, a gentle young man speaking soft words. She was floating on the scent and the language and the touch of the breeze on her skin.

So far. And to a man ...

Not that she would ever have put flowers in her hair. Not when anyone could see. She would have been too embarrassed. And when was there such a smooth-faced and smooth-tongued young man? Her suitors were of a rougher mould. Except for Maurizio, her godmother's son. He had come to visit each time he was home from university. He brought flowers, sweets. It was understood. Only she had not acquiesced to the understanding, to his languishing glances or his moist, plump fingers casual and proprietorial on her arm. Even in the piazza, his hand around her shoulder or on her elbow, guiding. His words had been not so much smooth as spongy. Maria had felt she could sink into them without ever encountering a central core of meaning. "I don't understand. What do you mean?" she would say to Maurizio as they ambled on a Sunday afternoon walk.

And he would smile. "Well, you wouldn't."

Cesare, he had been different from the beginning, hard-edged in his straightforwardness. "I've come back to Italy to find a wife," he told her father on his first visit to the house. "I had a fiancée. That is, I thought I did. But when I returned, everything had changed. And I only have three weeks left." He had come to bring news of her oldest brother, who did not live in the same city as Cesare did but whom he knew nevertheless. "Two hundred miles is nothing there," he said. "The space – the room – it's fantastic."

If only she had understood then how "fantastic" it was. Of course, she hadn't been thinking at all at the time. How else could she explain it? She had looked at this dark, quick moving stranger in a too-tight suit and hair that stood straight up like a rooster, and she was dazed. He had the brightness of the sun at noon shining on the sea, hurting her eyes.

And the stranger, Cesare, watched her from across the room, and in two evenings he chose. "I was desperate. I had so little time left," he told not only her but all the *ragazzi* one Sunday dinner. "I had to have a wife. I couldn't return without one. I would have taken anyone. Even a whore if she was willing."

"That's the one thing she would be," Lucio said.

"Thank you. Such esteem," Maria said. She was too embarrassed to look at the others.

Cesare laughed and passed his hand roughly over her cheeks, in and out of her hair. "I am amazed that I was so lucky. My own little snowdrop."

"A mountain flower indeed," Lucio added.

"Special. And as pure –"

"Enough, Cesare."

He had chosen and she, well, she had found herself in the town hall, embarrassed by Cesare's shouting at the official who insisted that the papers couldn't be done on such short notice, mesmerized by his fist pounding the shiny desk. She found herself in her cousin's wedding dress, found herself repeating the hallowed words. And when Cesare was gone and she was released from the force of his choice and began to think, it was too late.

"I don't know him. He's a stranger and Canada is so far –"

"You will know him. After your years together, you'll know. And you are his wife. Before God."

His wife before God. Before. The child flailed. Before.

A sudden sharp sound. She lay still, waiting, her feet still up. What else could she do? But it was only Nico, lunchbucket in hand. She didn't like his seeing her so laid out, but to start thrashing around to get up would be worse. She had always felt more awkward with him than with Lucio or Mario or Beppi. He rarely said much, and the paucity of words together with his stockiness and jaw-heavy face gave him a sullen, hulking presence.

"Is there any mail?" It was always his first question. Though, of course, it was the primary concern of all the *ragazzi,* no matter how politely the others might first inquire after her health.

"Not for you. There's a letter for Beppi." She started to hoist herself to a sitting position. Nico did not offer a helping hand but continued to stare down at her. A bit irritated, she said without thinking. "It has been a long time since she wrote to you. Maybe you should start worrying."

His expression didn't change. "Twenty days." Finally he gave her his hand.

In the kitchen she began the supper preparations. She felt even more clumsy and misshapen than usual before him. Not that Nico was watching her. Each time she turned from the counter or sink, he was staring down at his hands. He had never sat with her before. Normally he stayed in his room. He had a record player and many 78s of operatic arias. He played them for hours, "Vesti la giubba" and "Addio Gloria." infiltrating the whole house. He did sit in the kitchen some evenings, but only when all the *ragazzi* were there. He liked to play cards and to harmonize on an impromptu song. He particularly liked to be coaxed into giving a solo. He had a good baritone voice with only a slight tendency to shout.

"I didn't know you used cans."

Maria nearly dropped a can of chicken broth. "I don't. Only what's natural and genuine, of course. Everything homemade. But now," she could feel her face flushing: "I can't stand the smell of broth cooking. Makes me ill. Tomato sauce too . . . You do understand? You won't say anything?"

Nico murmured an "of course" and went back to staring at his hands.

What did he want? She disliked cooking at the best of times, and being watched made it worse. Maria hadn't known how to cook when she got married. That first night in Edmonton, on top of her disappointment with the house, her shyness with Cesare, on top of her grief at leaving home, the crowning touch was the realization that she was expected to care and cook for not one man but five.

Cesare had noticed her expression. He immediately guided her into their bedroom and sat her down. "We can ask them to leave. It's up to you. I won't impose them on you." And when she didn't answer, "I know it's hard. I remember what it was like for me four years ago. Did I ever tell you that after the first six weeks, I made up my mind to go back? I thought cold country, cold people. It's not the place for me. I was on my way to buy a ticket home." His arm crept around her shoulder. "But Mario and Beppi, they walked all the way to the ticket office with me, trying to persuade me to stay. I was at the door when what they were saying began to sink in. Friends make all the difference in this place. You'll see. Surrounded as we are by strangers – just to come home and hear the sound of our dialect." He paused and turned her head so that she faced him. "It makes me feel not so far from home." His touch on her face was assertive. "And they do pay well. It's a way for you to help, help us to get home faster."

At the end of the three days she had asked for in which to decide, she told Cesare that they could stay. It did not take much to understand that otherwise, with Cesare working at two jobs, she would be almost always alone. The *ragazzi* helped keep the ice from her heart. The teasing, the laughter and the songs were insulation against the winter winds.

"We thought you were *in servizio,*" Mario had said quite soon after she arrived. "We counted on it."

"I was." Maria was indignant. "But I never cooked. I was the children's nursemaid. I was in service to the Count and Countess Mironna. I certainly wasn't expected to cook."

"What about at home?" Beppi asked.

"My stepmother did it all. And before her, my older sister . . . I was never interested."

"Oh ho!" Mario, as usual, was smiling. "And what feasts we dreamt of. When Cesare told us you were coming. Such banquets. After my days in that wretched house with only a hotplate. I thought what luck. Now – now – everything will be put right. Cesare, you should have thought of this. Given each prospective bride a cooking test."

They had all laughed. Except Maria. Though it didn't take her long to see that it was no use getting offended. They did, indeed, need those meals, reproducing as closely as possible what they had eaten at home.

Lucio, the one with the best profile and the big dark eyes, gave her lessons in the basics: broth, minestrone, sauce, and so on. He spoke Italian with her rather than the dialect he used with the others, and that, together with his deliberate, slow movements and his formal manner, "now one measures out," gave a ritualistic tone to those lessons. The slicing, the frying, the boiling, *the* preparation of the meal.

"I've been laid off." Again Nico's words, after the long silence, startled her. He was staring at her, waiting for a response.

"It's so cold working outside now. Maybe it's for the best. You have enough stamps for unemployment, don't you?"

"Barely enough. But, you see, the less I earn the longer

until I can ask Paola to marry me." His cheeks were flushed. "I'm tired of waiting . . . I need a wife."

The need for a wife, Nico, Beppi, Mario, Lucio, they all came back to that, over and over. At home, they had mothers, aunts, sisters, friends. There were ex-schoolmates and the girls that walked the *passeggiata* in the evening. But here, except for Maria, their daily lives were womanless. They ogled any girl they saw, of course; there was a convent school near the house and Mario, in particular, would stand beneath the dormitory windows and call up. But there was never any real contact. And they had not been raised to be the type of men who went to whores, not unless they were desperate. A wife – she could replace all the women each felt he had lost. She could take care of and care for him, certainly; but more, she could save him from losing himself in this land of indifferent eyes. Woman, she could protect him from the brute state he felt he could be so easily reduced to: beast of burden, lust-filled animal.

That evening as, with Lucio's help, she cleared the table, they began again. Beppi was smoking and complaining, complaining and smoking. Gina, his fiancée, had announced that she wouldn't come to Canada unless he promised that they would stay no longer than five years. "Ridiculous. Five years. And she expects me to sign a legal document. No trust."

"At least she writes to you. At least you have it fixed. You and Lucio are the lucky ones." Nico poured himself another glass of wine.

Mario picked three oranges from the fruit bowl still on the table. Pushing his chair back a bit, he began to juggle and hum the old song, "Femmena."

"Paola doesn't write anymore. I'm just fooling myself . . ." Nico was drawing the bottle towards him again.

Mario missed an orange. It fell . . . plaff. "I may have the solution for you." He kept on juggling with the remaining two. "Did you notice that little dark-eyed sweetie in church the last two Sundays?" He had all their attention now. "Tiny. Brown hair. White coat?"

"I thought she was here to marry one of the Neapolitans."

"She was. But she'd never met the groom. And when she got here and saw him, she refused to go through with it."

"I don't see how this can help me. How do you know anyway?"

Mario was easing himself into a standing position, still juggling.

Maria began to bend over to pick up the orange. Her stomach tightened as it had many times in the past week. This time, there was an undertow of pain.

"The supposed brother-in-law-to-be works with me at the packing plant. He's indignant of course."

"But why," Beppi asked, "would she be interested in Nico?"

"So pretty," Lucio added.

"Think. She's from the South. If she went back, there'd be a scandal."

"But how would I start? How would I approach her? And if she's picky . . . Where's she staying?"

Mario began to dance around the table. He swivelled his hips and pretended the oranges were mariachis.

Ma tu sei guaglione.
Non conosci femmena.

Her abdomen tightened again, and again there was pain. "I have to lie down."

They all focussed on Maria. "Are you tired?"

"Do you think it's starting?"

"What's wrong? You're very pale."

"Your stomach?"
"It's not time yet, is it?"
"I thought the spring."
"Cesare said late March."
"What is it?"
"I don't know. I don't know what it's supposed to feel like. No one told me. I don't know."
"Call Cesare."
"It comes and goes."
"That's it. I'm sure of it. Go, Lucio, phone."
"Some brandy?"
"Idiot . . . Maria, breathe deeply."

Her whole body was clenching. The *ragazzi* were still asking questions, their voices a background roar. She was frozen to her chair, unable to move.

Her runaway heart was speeding, the blood pressing against the pain. If she could run away, if she could escape the pain that came not from within but without, escape the alien force that was squeezing, squeezing the baby out. If she could get home, if she could see her father's eyes, faded and blue, if she could smell . . .

"So far and to a man I don't know."

Cesare was with her now, his eyes wide with emotion. "Calm. Stay calm," he kept saying in a sharp, loud voice. He rammed her feet into his boots, pushed her arms into his parka. He was still so unexpected, so strange to her.

"You will know him."

Papa, no, Mamma. It was her mother's eyes, those first eyes that she needed. Though she could not remember them, not as they were. When she tried to conjure them, she saw the steady gaze of a black and white photograph. She could recall her presence, her arms and lap, being held in a darkened room. But that was all.

To call Mamma was to long to see again the well-tended grass in the cemetery on the hill behind the village, to long for the scent of oleanders Mamma, she had been told, planted along the front of their house. To call Mamma was to long for the primary comfort that should have been.

In the car Maria shivered only partly with cold. She stared out at the dirtied streets. "What do they do with the coffins? Do they keep them stacked up somewhere?"

"What do you mean?"

She gestured at the piles of snow in the yards, glinting under the streetlights. "The land is too hard. How could they dig a hole?" She wanted to say more, much more, but she held back. Cesare was so quick to anger, and she didn't want to be called *stupida*, not again.

In fact, Cesare did not answer her. He kept staring straight ahead. Only after the next pain, when she had forgotten that she had said anything, did he glance at her. "Everything will be fine. We're not in your village now. And you are not your mother." The words and the voice, a quiet voice he had never used before, broke through to her.

For the first time, she began to cry before him. "I'm afraid."

"No need."

"I'll . . . I can't do it."

"Of course you can." Then, in a different tone: "Come, we're here. It's time to go in."

"Time . . ." Maria stared at the brightly lit emergency entrance. Cesare opened her door and extended an arm. She didn't move. He reached in and pulled at her legs.

In the last months the house and the car had both imprisoned and protected her. Now, outside containment, in the moments of unrelieved winter and in the many hours of corridors and hospital rooms, she was exposed. She had already lost much that she was in leaving home. Now the nurses took away her clothes; they sent away Cesare; a small blond one unlatched her fingers from his arm. They prodded and palpitated. They gestured and jabbered. The small one flashed a long rubber hose in front of Maria's eyes. She was commanding her to do something but what? Her pursed little mouth barked at the aide. Immediately, hands were upon Maria, shoving her to the side, spreading her buttock cheeks. She had been crying silently but could no longer hold back. "Mamma," she called, "Mamma." Being helped to the toilet, being washed, being shaved, two aides holding her, one on each leg. "Mamma."

"Shush," said the blond nurse, her freckled face scrunched in disgust. "Italians!"

Maria understood that. She wished she had the strength to sit up and punch her in her flat stomach. She did try and lift a leg. But now the nurse was talking to someone in the corner. The doctor floated into view. He was pulling on rubber gloves – inspecting. Not her face. He never looked at her face or into her eyes. He thrust his hand inside her. Big, he said over her stomach to the nurse and then something *spaghetti*.

But the pain was blotting out the room, the doctor and the nurse. It was tearing up time, tearing up any pause. It was tearing her apart. "Mamma," a prick on her arm and she no longer heard her own cries. More hands. "Mamma," she was whispering. The pain was no alien force. It was her very centre.

She was in another room with shiny walls. A bright light aimed at her eyes. The nurses were masked. And her doctor – she recognized his icy eyes though. Finally, she must be close to the end. A rubber mask was handed to her. She understood gas, a solid word in a stream of sounds.

The pain no longer possessed her. A still terror had beaten it off. A frozen sea, a still sky, icebergs. Where was this place? What was happening? She was floating in the icy whiteness. There was no up or down, no signposts and no sounds. Only the relentless white. And she was falling, slowly spiralling down, ever down. She thrashed against the fall, stretching her hands to catch onto anything that might be there. Where was she? More, who was she? But her mind was as white as the featureless world. She was lost.

But, as suddenly as the fall began, her hands were no longer grasping at air. She was holding something solid. The whiteness was separating into colours and shapes. She could make out murmurs, metallic sounds. Her baby was in her arms. Perfect to see, to smell, to touch. Maria's head was still spiralling, still confused, but her boy had grounded her. Indeed, though she was not to know it for many years, his pudgy body was her first connection to the hard, foreign land.

She was saved and she was bound.

Everlasting Life

And now, on the edge of death, Augusta did not change her ways.

"I want another pillow, farther up," she commanded.

"There . . . is that the way you want it, Mamma?"

"No, you stupid girl. I want it farther up. I told you."

"There?"

"Pull me up more. Not like that. Under the arms. Pull."

Patrizia braced herself and heaved Augusta into an upright position.

"Aghh," Augusta shrieked.

"Sorry . . ."

"With gentleness. I'm not a sack of potatoes."

Indeed not, Patrizia thought, Augusta was more resistant and awkward to move than even a hundred pounds of potatoes. "Sorry."

Patrizia shrank from her mother's heavy, shapeless flesh. She had to push herself to wash Augusta, to be scrupulous with each private fold, to massage cream onto her sore, mottled back, her twisted right hand or crusted feet. Patrizia felt that if she pulled a little too hard her mother's flesh would come away from the bone in purple lumps, then turn gelatinous in her hands.

Physically, the mother she had known survived only in remnants: certain facial expressions of disbelief or disdain, the timbre and tone of her voice, the lines of her long, severe face, blurred but still visible under the web of wrinkles. Her hair was still dark and thick and her eyes large and black. But now those eyes were like two mirrors, reflecting back the outer, but revealing no inner light.

Patrizia settled back on the chair beside her mother's bed. She lay her hand over Augusta's and smiled reassuringly. "Is that better, Mamma?" Augusta shook her head. "What's wrong? Are you thirsty?" Another shake of the head. "A pain? Are you in pain? I can get you a pill."

"No," her mother said to each and every one of Patrizia's questions. No, no, no. Augusta sighed loudly and closed her eyes. Patrizia's sigh was barely audible. She stared at the wall opposite, blank except for a turgidly-coloured picture of Christ, smiling sorrowfully and holding his bleeding heart in his hand. Anything, even that monstrosity, was better than gazing down at her mother hour after hour. She had been sitting this way for five long, long days. Ever since she had arrived in Sicily, called back after many years by her mother's illness. Five days. Seventeen left to go. The new trimester would be beginning. Two and a half weeks: surely, by then things would be resolved, one way or the other. She could not be expected to stay any longer. Her classes, her research, her life: they were all waiting for her.

Not that Augusta would understand. Even when she had had less need, she felt that children owed their mother everything. They had argued about it once when she had overheard Patrizia say "please" to one of her sons. "You do not ask a son or a daughter," Augusta said. "You tell them. A child owes his parent unquestioning obedience."

"My children owe me nothing," Patrizia said, "as far as owing goes."

A child owes her mother: obedience, respect, love, care, compassion. Augusta loved to enumerate. *To a mother*, she would pause dramatically, *to a mother who gave you life?* And she would lift her shoulders and her voice to express the magnitude of the duty. And Patrizia, she made clear, Patrizia did not live up to her most basic expectations.

Augusta herself had stopped living with her parents at sixteen and from then on, except for payments of conscience money, had conducted her life as if she were an orphan. Once years ago, Patrizia had used this against her mother, calling her a hypocrite. "You lived alone," she'd said. "You studied; you taught; you did it when women didn't do that, especially not in Palermo. And you deny me a tenth of that freedom."

Her mother had conceded nothing. "I did what I had to do," Augusta said. "It's not the same for you. You should be grateful." Grateful that she was born into the family that she was, grateful that, unlike Augusta, she didn't have parents that were little more than gypsies, travelling from place to place, on the fringes of society.

Patrizia did not remember her grandparents; both died during her infancy, and Augusta rarely spoke of them. But Patrizia was as proud of them as her mother was ashamed. She loved to tell people that her mother's family were Sicilian puppeteers, dramatizing the legends of Charlemagne's knights, the good Christians in battle with the evil Moors, tales of honour, courage and civility. "They carried the ancient songs, the epic poetry, village to village, all through the island and the South."

"Another pillow, higher up." Augusta's voice was commanding.

"Mamma, enough, you'll topple over."

"When will that idiot of a woman bring the *caffè latte*. I wait and wait for breakfast, and it never comes."

"Mamma, you just finished your lunch."

A faint flicker in those opaque eyes. "I have eaten then."

"Yes. Don't you remember?"

"No, I haven't eaten. Not for three days."

"You had *brodo* and *pastina*. And a soft-boiled egg. I fed you. Remember? You didn't want to take your pills. I had to beg you. Remember?"

This was a new loss: her sense of time gone. What was left? What could Augusta apprehend? She stared at the wall, but did she see it? Following each crack and curve, the advance and the retreat of light. The play of shadows. Or did scenes from the past block out the present? Wasn't that what was supposed to happen – on the edge of death? You relived your life.

Augusta gave no sign. Her eyes were closed, her head sagging sideways. Girlhood, womanhood, age, a rotation of light, a blur of colours, like the brightly painted wheel of the Sicilian cart. Patrizia let her eyelids drop. She could hear the roar of the crowd, the cheers, the hisses, the laughs, the applause. The clatter of sword on sword, the din of marionette battle, the intonation of the poetry, word linked to word in the compelling flow of *terza rima*, the voice of the father pitched high then low for the different roles (Orlando, Marsilio, Rinaldo, Agricane, the good and the bad), the mother singing a stately, regretful song. And Augusta, a pretty little girl in a pretty red dress posed before a decorated donkey and a Sicilian cart, Augusta, calling out to the passing throng, come in, come in, thinking we need more, we need more, for supper, for the night, come in, come in and hear the songs of women and knights, of arms and love, of courtesy.

Patrizia loosened her mother's grasp gently, finger by finger. She had to wipe her hands, her face of the sweat, which she did quickly, putting her hand back before her mother called for it. It was hot and close in the small, white room in spite of the height of the ceiling and the thickness of the walls. If she opened the shutters there was a chance of a breeze. But that would also let in the din of the Vespas and cars beeping their way along. The sounds that came through the open door from the kitchen were enough. The kitchen was the main room used by Giuseppina, the woman who owned the house, her daughters, and, it seemed, an infinite number of fat women identified as relatives or friends. Most of the other rooms and the entire second floor were left to the three genteel, well-off ladies who paid highly for Giuseppina's care.

Patrizia wouldn't have chosen this place for her mother. When her brother had brought mother and father back to Sicily at their insistence, there weren't many options. The three nursing homes in the area all had long waiting lists. "It will take several years," he was told. Both he and Patrizia had been gone too long to have any connections to a person with influence, who could make things happen. "Well," Roberto had said, "She's eighty-eight. How long could she have left?"

"Patrizia!" It was a frightened cry.

"Yes, Mamma. I'm here . . . Do you want something?"

"I don't remember."

"A drink of water?"

"I'm always confused. My poor head."

"No. Don't think that way. The more you convince yourself that you're confused, the more confused you will become. Try and think, 'My mind is clear. I can understand.' "

"My mind is clear," Augusta repeated, but with wonder and doubt.

Suddenly Patrizia's mouth was full of sour saliva and her hands were trembling. Her mother's condition was her own fault. Augusta had been weakened as much by the relaxing of her will as by the various illnesses. Ten years ago – after a minor stroke – she had let go. "I'm tired," she declared. And refused to walk again. But even as Patrizia was swept with anger, she knew that she was being ridiculous. Old age could not be fought with will or understanding.

Those had always been Patrizia's weapons. She had shaped her life through her will and understanding; she had escaped the solid, respectable Sicilian life of her parents for a freer, more fluid life in California. And though her mother, with the same intensity of will, had strained in the opposite direction, lifting herself out of bohemia into the aristocratic, land-owning class of her husband, Augusta had stopped there, stopped choosing, stopped growing.

"One must make choices responsibly, in good faith," Patrizia would warn her students. "One must try to discern which side is the side of life." Slipping the advice into her introduction of *Orlando Furioso* for her Italian Renaissance literature classes. "For we are all tested, not through literal duels, but through equivalent tests of our honour, courage and civility."

Even as a teenager, Patrizia had understood that her parents were not alive but clay marionettes manipulated by their anger and resentment towards each other into repeating the tragicomedy of wandering husband and disgusted wife over and over again. She first tried to escape the bitter scenes, the endless recriminations by running away at fourteen, getting as far as Naples where the police caught her. At eighteen she decided to marry, but leaving home wasn't enough. If she stayed in Sicily, somnolent, unchanging Sicily, she too would be transformed from woman to marionette, her flesh fired into clay by that oven of history, heat and custom. So she persuaded Carlo to emigrate to the new world, although it was rare for a middle class Sicilian to do so. They'd gone to America to be free, and it was only years later that she understood that they had brought their strings with them. They were caught in a tragicomedy of their own.

"I'm thirsty." Augusta seemed to be addressing the wall rather than Patrizia.

"Here." Patrizia poured the water from bottle to glass. "Here." She held up the glass and with her free hand, gently guided Augusta's face to the glass.

"Ugghh. Poison."

"Signora." One of Giuseppina's twin daughters in her usual jeans stood at the door.

"Yes, Barbara."

The girl lowered her head and lifted her eyes in a parody of shyness. "My mother wants you to come."

As Patrizia disentangled her hand and got up, her mother cried out. "So, you're leaving me?"

"No, Mamma. I'll be right back. I must go and speak with Giuseppina."

"A mother," Augusta said. "Me, a mother."

"A minute, Mamma, a minute."

The kitchen was overwhelming after the quiet of the white room. In a corner, the twins each stirred a different pan on the stove and sang along to an American pop song blaring from the transistor on the fridge. Across the room, Signora Miralda lay on a red canvas cot and talked softly to herself. Giuseppina, an enormous woman in the requisite black dress, sat at the table in a blue-velvet armchair, chatting loudly in Sicilian to an equally enormous woman with a glass eye in a straight-back chair.

"Come, Signora." Giuseppina shouted at her. "Come, sit. Please," motioning to another stuffed chair at the end of the table.

"Thank you." Patrizia paused to greet Signora Miralda and squeeze her trembling hand .

"So," Giuseppina was still shouting, "are you still considering calling in another doctor?"

"I have. Called in another one. He's coming after his office hours."

"Who? Who did you call? Don't you trust our doctor? He saw your father through. And he's been visiting your mother all this last year. He knows her."

"Of course I do. No, I called the doctor from Balestrate. He's an old friend so . . . A second opinion never hurts."

"We have had full responsibility for your mother. If you are dissatisfied –" Giuseppina shrugged her enormous shoulders.

"No, no, please don't misunderstand me. It's just my mother doesn't –" Patrizia stopped, suddenly unsure of what she was about to say. Fortunately everyone (even Miralda, head shaking) had switched their attention to the tiny old woman in the doorway. Patrizia guessed her to be the Signora Margherita she had never seen, since the lady never descended from the second floor, but whose footsteps she'd often heard these last five days, back and forth, over and over.

"What now? It's always something. Never any peace." Giuseppina muttered as she hauled herself up and out of the chair. "Will you turn that damn radio off?" She was back to her normal shout. "We can't hear ourselves think. Signora Margherita, such a surprise. You wanted something?" She grabbed the old woman by the elbow, but Margherita shook the massive hand off and inched her way to the centre of the room, leaning on a carved walking stick.

"Signora, is something wrong?"

When Margherita reached the table, she dropped the stick and manoeuvred herself into position, one hand on the table, the other palm outward, pressed to her forehead so that her full black sleeve curtained her face. "Is something wrong? When has it ever been right?" Her voice was surprisingly gentle and young. She did not alter her Eleanor Duse, silent-movie pose. "In this life of filth and pain . . ." Patrizia's throat was suddenly tight. She ran her tongue hard over her teeth to control the flare of hysteria.

Margherita dropped her arm. "When could it ever have been right when we spend our time submerged beneath putridness and the blood of our fellow man?" Her glassy blue eyes focussed into two clear pin-pricks of light. She pointed a short wrinkled finger at Patrizia. "Life, you must understand, is not worthy of being lived."

Everyone else, even the twins, nodded in tragic agreement. Pessimism was a given in Sicily, a cliché everyone paid allegiance to, and statements on the universality of suffering were recited as frequently as Have-a-nice-day was in California. Still, Margherita's expressions were more extreme than most.

"Life is what you make it," Patrizia found herself saying in her professorial voice. "If one makes choices responsibly . . ."

Margherita leaned closer, so she was face to face with Patrizia, and her smell, both sharp and mouldy, engulfed Patrizia. "I may be blind," she said in Sicilian, "but this one is blinder."

"Yes, yes." Giuseppina said, signaling to Patrizia with a shake of her head. "But what was it that you wanted."

Margherita lowered herself into the chair one of the twins had placed behind her. "I told you yesterday. Usually the funerals pass by Via Libertà, and I watch them from my window. But the one today is a much more important one. I forget the man's name."

"Inteso. Don Mario Inteso," Giuseppina offered.

"Whatever." Margherita's hand fluttered through the air. "Important funerals always go by Via Garibaldi. You should know that by now, Giuseppina. So I had to come down to see it. I thought I'd watch from the door."

"Don Mario was a man of honour." Giuseppina rolled her eyes heavenward in the required fashion. "I don't care what they say. A man of honour. He did all he could for my Vito. If it hadn't been for those bastards – may all their children spit on their graves –Vito would be here with us right now. Don Mario tried. Not openly, of course. But he tried. In the old days it wouldn't have been like this. Before these new turds that call themselves magistrates."

Patrizia concentrated on not showing her disdain. "My Vito would have been with us now. A father to the daughters who need him. Need him like the bread they eat – especially now that they are reaching that dangerous age when they need vigilance..." Giuseppina continued but Patrizia stopped listening. She had heard the proud story of Vito the saint before. She had been away from Sicily too long to accept that a man who was part of a kidnapping plot and who managed to collect a hefty ransom before he was caught could be a "good man." True she had heard that the victim was lieutenant of a gang that was trying to muscle into Inteso's territory. Still, a kidnapping was a kidnapping. Besides, Giuseppina seemed to think Vito was a saint because he had managed to keep part of the ransom, transforming it into expensive embroidered sheets for his daughters' dowries, a new bathroom for the house, and three hundred and eighty-five sheep.

Sheep – Patrizia suddenly remembered – sheep, last night in her dream. And her lungs contracted. She lit a cigarette to keep herself breathing. She could see and feel slices of the dream. A stone road wound up a green hill. At the top of the hill stood a ruined Greek temple of golden stones. Though she walked and walked, she got no farther up the hill. Abruptly, the temple disappeared. A phalanx of sheep was running down the hillside toward her. Then they had her, butting her with their long, black snouts, pinning her arms and legs. She could not see. Her mouth was forced open to accept the greasy wool. She was choking.

Across the table, Giuseppina's friend was staring at her, the good eye neutral, the darker glass one glaring.

"*Signora*," Giuseppina was also staring at her. "Please. Would you like something? More coffee?"

"Yes." Patrizia rose. "Coffee. Could you bring it to the room please?"

"And a little sandwich? You barely touched your lunch."

"No. Thank you. As I told you before, I never eat much."

"A slice of *cassata?*""

"Heavens, no . . . Thank you."

"Some chocolates?"

"No. Really." This was getting to be a distorted replay of scenes, many years ago, between herself and her mother. At least Giuseppina was not likely to lock her in her room. Of course, the real question was whether the woman was as attentive and as insistent in her care of Augusta or whether this was only a show, performed to reassure.

"Aren't you going to watch the funeral pass? It should be here soon," Signora Margherita said to Patrizia, who had risen. "There's going to be over thirty cars, all covered in flowers, purple and white, of course, and a hundred official mourners."

"No. I think not. I had better close this door too. In case the wailing bothers my mother."

"Just two more minutes and it will be here. You could learn something."

"Two minutes!" A shriek from one of the twins.

"I'm supposed to go to Maria's. I've got to get going before . . ." Her charge across the room was blocked when she passed the table. Her mother's hand clamped down around her right arm.

"What do you think you're doing?"

"She has the new Madonna tape . . . And she asked a few friends. Ma, let go. O.K. I should have asked. But I thought it was no big deal. Everyone's going."

"Not everyone," commented the other twin at the stove.

"I know Maria and her harebrained parents. When you say 'everyone,' you mean there'll be boys there."

"So . . ."

"So! What would your father say? So what will the people say if you start consorting with that group? Stupid hussies. You have to be careful – both of you –more than the other girls. You have to think of our name, our reputation."

What would people say? The phrase had been an answer to everything from why Patrizia couldn't study medicine to why she couldn't be allowed to make her own bed. She felt a surge of yearning for her anonymous California city where she did not even know the names of her closest neighbours.

"I don't care what they say. I'm going."

Both Giuseppina and her daughter were shouting now. Signora Margherita stopped on her labourious way to the door, turning to Patrizia. "Cut the balls off all the males and shove corks up all the females. It's the solution to everything."

"But, Signora, wouldn't that lead to the end of mankind?"

"What do you think I've been trying to tell you?"

The exchange fuelled Patrizia's smile all the way back to the doorway of her mother's room. There the sight of Augusta, all purple and yellow and disjointed, on the white bed in the white room, tensed her face back into its habitual concerned expression. The bed was so narrow and the room so empty and her mother so solitary, lying there like a forgotten toy. And when, sensing a presence, Augusta turned her face to the doorway, her eyes were intelligent with fear.

"Mamma."

"Ahhh . . . Patrizia." Vacancy clouded over the fear. Whom had she expected with such trepidation? Surely Giuseppina wouldn't deserve such a reaction? Or had there been subtle mistreatments Patrizia hadn't yet discovered? "Finally. Such a long time. Come here. By me . . . Here."

"One minute, Mamma. Just one more minute. I forgot something."

She insisted on speaking to Giuseppina in the hall where the Signore, the daughters, and the glass-eyed friend couldn't overhear. "I know you told me that she never asks where he is or what happened. But does she ever mention him, ever allude to him at all?"

"No. Like I said. She chatters about you and your brother, even about Signorina Santa. But not a word about Don Vittorio. It's like she never knew him."

Patrizia dropped wearily into the chair by the bed, returning her hand to her mother's grasp. Why had she looked so afraid? Obviously, for a moment, she hadn't recognized Patrizia. Was the fear because of that lack of recognition of who stood at the door? Or was it anticipatory terror at someone in particular? The angel of death? The return of Don Vittorio? Had she really forgotten the man she had slept beside for fifty years? Or was she pretending that she had forgotten, pretending so as to obscure the relief she felt at finally being free of him? The bitterness between them, the bitterness that was at least as long as Patrizia had memory, had not dissipated in old age. When they had come to live with her in California, they had continued their tragicomedy: her father hobbling after the black cleaning woman, one hand offering candies, the other positioning itself for a feel; her mother railing, her voice a hysterical croak.

Augusta's head jerked down suddenly, waking her from her doze. "Ai . . ." Her eyes, this time, were vague. "Aiiih . . ."

"Is it the pain again? It is time for another pill. Past time. Let me pour you some water. There. Yes, a bit more. You will be better soon. Lean back. That's right."

"You're a good girl, Patrizia. A saint . . . a saint." Augusta drifted back to sleep.

Saint: another name to add to the list she had used for her daughter over the years. The others had been equally inaccurate but more difficult to accept. Especially in the time before she had married Carlo. Even a request to be allowed to be alone with him for one hour, one week before the wedding, brought forth a torrent of abuse. In the end, Don Vittorio had been uncharacteristically firm and insisted Patrizia be allowed her car ride with Carlo.

Patrizia never understood her mother's reaction, extreme even for a Sicilian mother, just as she never understood the greater mystery of how the link between two people such as her parents had come about. Not until a seemingly senile mutter, so unrelated to the conversation at the time that she'd nearly ignored it, illuminated both areas of incomprehension. "Your brother was late. He wasn't premature at all." A passion had burned for a short time between Augusta and Vittorio, a passion that could have dishonoured the puppeteer's daughter as many less determined recipients of the Don's love had been and were to be dishonoured.

And Augusta had feared that Patrizia would be tainted with the shame that Augusta had avoided. Ironically, she viewed the alternative – marriage – just as darkly. "I hate weddings," Augusta would say whenever the subject came up.

Don Vittorio had always been a gentle and a generous man; Patrizia felt indignation at her mother's seeming forgetfulness, at her implied fear. Indignation yet kinship. Carlo was, Patrizia had to admit, a good man and a devoted husband. But when Carlo was finally gone – after weeks of trying to make him understand that she wanted no more of marriage, after weeks of finding herself answering exhortations and tears with declamations about freedom, truth and responsibility to self like some George Sand heroine – her whole body loosened. She rediscovered the ability to move without jerks, to turn her head without a sudden block.

"A saint. A saint." Augusta spoke in her sleep.

Yet, despite the new freedom of movement, she still was not free. Although she hired a woman to care for her parents, her mother called for her constantly. "Where are you going? When will you be home? Work, you are always saying you're going to work. I don't believe you. You're a liar. Stay with us. Stay."

After Carlo left, Don Vittorio would check on her, dragging his slow body down the stairs in the middle of the night only to walk into her bedroom and say, "so you are here." Or thinking he had successfully hidden himself behind the dieffenbachia in the hall, he would poke his head around a leaf and gaze sorrowfully at her while she tried to entertain a male friend.

Finally, she informed her brother that he had to do something. "I need to be alone. I can't continue this way. It's your turn."

And he answered as she expected him to. "I can't take them. You remember how horrible it was for Anita last time. It's impossible, really impossible. But don't worry. I understand. I'll start looking into the nursing homes here." Patrizia balked at the thought of Don Vittorio and Donna Augusta, speaking no English, habituated to deference and years of an aristocratic life, in a nursing home in Tulsa, Oklahoma.

A solution presented itself. Don Vittorio began to repeat insistently that he must go home. "I cannot die in exile. I cannot die in this place." And he was so frail and so weak and Augusta, frailer and weaker, that Patrizia accepted that this was their final wish. She told herself that it could only be a question of a few months.

In his Christmas break, her brother had brought them back to Sicily and, after some inquiry, settled them at Giuseppina's. Patrizia began to breathe in the new silence, breathe in the empty house free of presences. It was so good to return at the end of a tiring day to find no one waiting for her, no one demanding that she begin his day. Still, sometimes the emptiness was inside her too. "Empty nest," her therapist said, "Parents, sons, husband, all gone. It'll pass." Though it hadn't, not yet. It had grown since her father died a short month after their return home.

While Augusta, the frailer, hung on.

Patrizia could hear her mother's voice across the years. *To a mother, who gave you life?* "It doesn't work in reverse. And I have a duty to myself. I have to go on living," she told her mother, still sleeping with her mouth open and saliva trickling down a purple crease.

"To go on living is not always the right choice in this stinking world." The voice came from the doorway, from a white triangular mask floating in blackness. "I knocked but you didn't hear me." It was Signora Margherita, a black gauze scarf draped over her head. "I became bold and entered. Hoping not to disturb."

"Come in. Would you like a chair?"

Signora Margherita shook her head. "I've been sitting all this time watching the funeral procession. It was exquisite." Patrizia glanced nervously back. Unfortunately, Augusta had wakened and hauled herself to a sitting position. "Each car was decked with enormous garlands of purple, white, and green flowers, and the hearse . . ."

"Please . . ." Patrizia motioned towards her mother, who was sinking, more yellow-faced than usual, back into the pillows. "Don't speak of these things here."

Margherita took several shuffling steps forward. She stretched her neck, cocked her head and took a long, hard look at Augusta. She lifted her shoulders in a shrug. "Whatever you say. Besides, this was not my purpose in introducing myself into the Signora's room this way. No, not my purpose at all."

"Excuse me?"

"I have heard that you have a supply of pills," Margherita said.

"Pills?"

"To make you sleep. You take one every evening."

Patrizia's lips were suddenly numb. Had they been spying on her? "Giuseppina has good eyes."

"Oh that one gets into everything, she does. You have to be vigilant. She enters my room when I'm sleeping. She throws my private things down, down on the floor. Can you imagine? She pretends it wasn't her, but . . ."

"Are you having trouble sleeping?"

"It is the eternal sleep that I search for. You know, no doubt, my history – the tragedy of my life with my brute of a husband."

"I have heard."

"And the filthy disease he inflicted on me?"

"I've heard that you believe –"

"Believe! We're not speaking of belief here." Margherita had gradually edged her way to Patrizia's side. "This is the truth; this is life that I'm telling you." Margherita waved her arm to emphasize her point, releasing her sharp, musty smell. "He inflicted his disease on me. Inflicted. What I could tell you about men. Not that you would listen. People don't. Except to their genitals. Oh, I know only too well. I am old now. I long for death. It has only been my cowardice – I detest pain – that has prevented me so far . . . To swallow some pills, fall asleep and never wake. It seems so clean, so tidy."

"And you expect me to give you some of my pills?"

"As an act of mercy. To help end my long agony. And no one need know that you helped."

"Your doctor . . ."

"Refuses to prescribe such pills. Signora, please, an act of mercy. God will bless you for it." Margerita's trembling hand was clutching Patrizia's shoulder. Patrizia resisted the impulse to slap her hand away, to push Margherita back. "To fall asleep . . ."

"It wouldn't work. Even if I could give you the pills, which I can't. Do you think Giuseppina could allow you to overdose? Imagine what people would say. It would reflect on her and her house. She'd only have you rushed off to the hospital. They stick tubes into you and pump out your stomach. It's most painful and most unpleasant."

"Well said, Signora." It was Giuseppina herself at the door, wiping the sweat from her forehead with a black handkerchief. "Exactly right." She waddled over to Margherita. "I wondered what you got up to. Went all the way up to your room and – nothing. Come on now. You're very tired. Too much excitement. Not good for you. Come on. Moment my back's turned, and you're up to mischief. What a life." Giuseppina had a hand on each of Margherita's tiny shoulders and was propelling her through the doorway when suddenly Patrizia's Aunt Santa appeared and blocked the way.

The two old women nearly collided. At the last moment, Giuseppina managed to tilt Margherita to one side and push her around the tremulous Santa. "Excuse me, excuse me," Giuseppina yelled.

"Help me." Margherita said. "Help me."

Zia Santa had not changed much in the years since Patrizia had last seen her or, for that matter, in the years since Patrizia's childhood. She was more dried out, had fewer teeth and walked bent over so that her chin was not much higher than her waist, but she had always looked old, all leathery skin and bones, a husk of a woman. When she and Patrizia exchanged kisses of greeting, she even felt like paper, crinkly and fragile in Patrizia's hands. "I have desired to see you for many days," Santa said, after she had finished bestowing the ritual kisses and greetings on Augusta. "But with this terrible flu in the air, I thought it best to stay in."

"That was wise."

"One can't be too careful at my age." Santa had always been careful, cleaning everything, including the plates, with rubbing alcohol. Her apartment had always been asphyxiating. "Look at your poor mother." Santa leaned forward and whispered close to Patrizia's ear. "She's close to the end, isn't she?" And together they gazed down at Augusta who stared blankly back at them.

"The doctor says the situation is critical," Patrizia whispered back.

"We must pray to our Father in heaven." The words sprayed out between Santa's remaining top five teeth onto Patrizia's cheek. "Poor Augusta. To the Blessed Virgin, to Saint Anthony, patron of lost causes. Pray."

"Every day she is a bit worse. Though she did recognize me immediately."

"The last two months, she has been insisting that you were coming to take her home." Santa paused for Patrizia's reaction, smiling slightly and clasping the large silver crucifix hanging from her neck.

"So you said on the phone."

"Each time I came to visit. Patrizia's coming, she would say."

"I hope you explained that I have a very busy life."

"She told me that you were important. And that's why you had to leave her here. Poor Augusta."

Patrizia made an effort to change the subject. "How do you find me, Zia? It's been twenty years. Have I changed much? I'm older, of course."

Santa switched her hand from her crucifix to her heavy black skirt. "It's hard to say what you are like now, seeing you dressed like a man. You were always a contrary one. Had to do things your way. I remember you holding your breath until you turned blue once, all because your mother wouldn't let you draw on the walls. From what I hear, you haven't changed much in that."

"Dressed like a man? Women wear slacks here too."

"The devil's conquering the entire world."

"What is she saying?" Augusta asked Patrizia.

"She's speaking of the devil, Mamma."

"Always the same," Augusta told the ceiling.

Giuseppina's glass-eyed friend entered with a tray of pastries.

"I made a special trip to the bakery on Via Manzoni," Santa said. "He makes the best *cannoli* in town. Since the nuns stopped."

"How thoughtful, Zia. I haven't had a *cannolo* in years."

"I want them." Augusta was pointing at the tray. "Yes, yes, yes," she said.

Giuseppina's friend lowered the tray so that it floated in front of Augusta's face. Augusta lunged, grabbing two pastries with her one working hand.

"Mamma, let me." Patrizia tried to loosen her mother's

grip, but Augusta only clutched harder. Cream dripped through her fingers onto the bedcover.

"Oh dear, oh dear, oh dear," said Santa.

Augusta brought her hand to her mouth. She took a large bite, managing to smear cream on both cheeks. She began to lick her fingers. Cream spread to her chin.

Giuseppina's friend had stayed, leaning her bulk against the window shutters and watching Patrizia mop up with kleenexes and a spare towel. "I have a book," she said suddenly, just as Santa opened her mouth to speak, "a book that is a witness to truth."

"You know how to read?" Santa was annoyed. "You're not illiterate?"

"What do you take me for?" The woman pulled herself up and took a position in the centre of the room.

"What is the truth?" Patrizia kept her voice polite.

"If each one of us accepts Jesus Christ as our personal saviour, we will never die."

"By all the saints in heaven," Santa nodded at the picture of Christ on the wall behind the woman and crossed herself, "by the Sacred Heart of Jesus, are you preaching to me? Me, of all people. Do you have any idea how many hours a day I spend on my knees?"

"Each one of us must, as I did, give up all idolatry, all false images. Each one of us must repudiate the whore of Rome." The woman's good eye gleamed with fervour.

"The whore of Rome?" Santa rolled her eyes at Patrizia. "Now, I know a couple of whores here in Alcamo. But Rome? I don't know anyone from Rome. So repudiating a particular whore would be meaningless."

"We must be reborn."

"Wasn't once enough?" asked Santa.

"You don't understand. I was born again. I was baptized in Lake Ontario."

"You don't need to go to some God-forsaken lake to be baptized. You can get it done at San Nicolo's at the corner."

"Three hundred of us – submerged and surfacing to everlasting life."

"Three hundred of you? Must have been a big lake. Were you all naked?"

"Dressed. Dressed." The woman was indignant.

"Well, praise the Lord for that at least."

Patrizia, who was feeding her mother the pastry a small bit at a time, could hold back no longer; she began to laugh. "What is it?" Her mother pulled at her hand. Patrizia shook her head. Tears were streaming down her cheeks.

"She's laughing at me, Signora. A poor Christian woman, trying to bring eternal life to those clinging to the death of sin."

"Not at all," Patrizia managed to gasp. "It's just my aunt..."

Santa smiled a gooey smile between bites of pastry. "Don't be offended, poor Christian. A sweet?"

The woman shook her head sadly on her way to the door. "You are not among the chosen."

"We're Sicilians, like everyone else," was Santa's reply.

Augusta gasped, then let out a sudden rattling wheeze. Patrizia turned back quickly to her, the laughter freezing in her throat. But her mother was smiling. "More *cannoli* for me?"

Santa pulled her chair closer to the bed. "Saint Anthony is a miracle worker. Doesn't she look better?"

"She does." There was a trace of fresh colour in her face.

"If I know my sister-in-law, I'd say she hasn't given up."

"No." Augusta was still eyeing the tray. "No," Patrizia said.

"Are you going to leave her here?"

"Before I came, I thought she was well cared for."

"They tend to her."

"Ah yes. Still, it's not quite . . . what with the kidnapped sheep and all."

"Thinking of taking her back to America? Back with you?"

"I don't know." But, as she felt herself tightening, she did.

ISLAND OF THE NIGHTINGALES

I escaped to the island. I ran away from the confusion, the murkiness, of my life to the simplicity of sun and sea.

Or so I told myself. It was the thing to do then – in the early 1970s – you left home, you escaped, to find or lose yourself. My friends backpacked across Europe; they travelled the overland route to Afghanistan or did drugs on a beach in Goa. They joined cults in Oregon or communes in the Kootenay valley. I claimed my *search* led me to Lussino, the long thin island parallel to the Dalmatian coast that was once the favourite resort of the Hapsburgs and the biggest island in the Adriatic – until the Romans dug a channel that divided it into two. I suggested that my arrival on those rocky shores sprang from some mysterious but inspired impulse while, actually, Lussino was my mother's hometown. The Lanzas had lived there for four centuries before they were exiled: picked up by a raging wind and blown across the world, to Australia and Canada, to America and Italy.

I was sent to Lussino, sent to stay with my great aunt. My parents thought a dose of village life would fortify me, like the bitter herbal tonic I took in the winter. Besides, it was a family tradition. Whenever a member of the younger generation had a problem, he or she was packed off not to a counsellor, but to another branch of the clan. A first cousin, who took up with an older man, was sent from Brisbane to an aunt in Queens. A second cousin in Long Island, who flunked first year university, was sent to my parents and the University of Calgary.

"You'll be able to get some perspective," my father said.

"See things clearly," said my mother. They were both hoping I would make up my mind. Papa wanted me to decide on a job, a career, a direction to my life. Mamma wanted me to choose between the two men I had been seeing.

"They are both crazy about you," she said, the way she had many times before – with pique and amazement.

Each morning I insisted on walking alone, telling my aunts that it helped me to think. I took the trail through the goat-scarred fields or the winding path through the orchards of fig trees or the paved way that ran over the cliffs bordering the sea. I was self-consciously playing the role of the runaway, alone, brooding, a contemporary version of the Victorian heroine: standing alone at the end of the pier, gazing enigmatically out to sea.

I did try to think. I had finished my Bachelor of Arts that spring and had automatically registered at graduate school. "As if that is going to get you anywhere," said my father. I contemplated law school and a teaching certificate. I imagined myself as a freelance writer in Toronto or a book editor in New York. I also tried to make a rational choice between Tony and Darryl. Was Darryl masterful or bossy? Was Tony loving or simply sappy? My pro and con lists for each man wavered and merged.

Besides, I was easily distracted by a view, a scent, the juxtaposition of red roofs, or a cluster of lemon trees. Like its two names, one Italian (Lussingrande) and one Croatian (Velilosinj), the place was both unfamiliar and familiar to me. I had visited the island only once – when I was five. The distractions were new, unremembered. I couldn't read the signs; Yugoslavia used the Cyrillic alphabet. I knew no Croatian: the language sounded impenetrable. I could grasp not even one word.

But I was raised amid images of Lussino: postcards on the

fridge, a blown-up photo of the piazza by the phone, a map of Dalmatia in my bedroom, and a painting of my mother's childhood home and garden over the fireplace. And I knew what those images represented to my mother: an eden of grapes and oranges, palms and figs; all that had been left behind, all that had been lost when the Lanzas were cast out after World War II by a punitive god or a so-called peace treaty. "You have no idea what it was like," she would say to me. "You are a lucky, lucky girl. Two suitcases, that's all I could take with me. Two miserable, battered suitcases."

For years, I had no patience with my mother's lamentations or her nostalgia. The old country, I would sneer, or point to a picture and say: a mediocre scene, nothing special. Now that I was on the island, I was more sympathetic. And if I didn't recognize the specifics of the place, I knew the idea of it.

I walked and my thoughts of jobs and men scattered. I walked and walked and lost my self-consciousness. I forgot the role I had given myself to play. I became dazed by the intensity of the midday heat, dazed by the sharp smell of the pine trees, dazed by the too bright sea.

Usually in the main piazza of the village there were a few hippies sprawled on the steps of the church, a mix of Italian and German tourists sitting at the two outdoor cafés that faced each other across the piazza, a sprinkling of locals – the men fixing their fishing nets in the quay, the women on their daily (and often futile) shopping expeditions. But that day, my third day of walking, when I reached the piazza, it swarmed with people, the majority of whom seemed to be young, well-dressed, and relaxed. I had to cross the piazza to reach the street of the *Osteria* where I had lunch, so I took a deep breath – and crowds always frighten me – and began threading my way around the chattering hives. I had just registered that the language being spoken was French when I heard a loud whoop coming from somewhere to my right. Turning, I found a curly-haired young man, dressed in wrinkled linen slacks and a shirt, staring at me. He began to whoop again, bouncing his palm off his thick lips. I turned back quickly, before I could be implicated, but in front of me there was another one, whooping. I tried going left, around him, but a third man blocked the way. I took one step back, then another. A casual withdrawal, I thought, an inconspicuous retreat. But on my next step, my foot came down not on cobblestones but on another foot. Two hands grabbed me around the waist, then began to move down, over my hips. I twirled, my arms flailing. The man let go but did not stand back. He stood close: his hand alternately covering and exposing a stretched mouth, large yellowish teeth, and a dark tongue.

I was surrounded, blocked on each side. They were making a dreadful noise with their mock cries, drawing the attention, I was sure, of the whole piazza. They moved their upper bodies forward and back rhythmically. I was not going to let them see my agitation. I stood still, imprisoned but unflinching at the centre of that tight circle of Europeans acting out their fantasy of an Indian war dance. With me as the captured maiden.

I was not going to scream.

I focussed on my feet, on the film of red dust clinging to the white sandal straps, dimming my pale toes. But at the edge of my vision I saw their sandalled feet, shuffling and stamping.

I would not scream. No. I looked up, past the shoulders of the savages to the terrace of the café. I fixed my sight on a woman sitting at one of the tables. It was amazing how clearly, how distinctly, I could see her. The savages were a blur before me. All my focus was on that woman. She was beautiful with waist-length black hair, a golden tan and high cheekbones; she was beautiful despite her aura of discontent. A man, fine-featured with dark hair and mustache, was sitting beside her. His whole body was angled towards her, and one of his hands encircled her wrist, hanging on. I knew that sort of manacling; it was all too familiar: the struggle for possession through containment.

I stared; the woman stared back. Then, shrugging slightly, she cupped her hands around her mouth. She seemed to be calling out to the savages. They were still dancing, still yelling. She stood up and leaned over the railing. I thought I heard a faint trace of her shout insinuating its way through the din. She was gesturing now. She caught the attention of the thick lipped one. He stopped his dance. He waved and smiled at her. The circle was finally falling away. Several of my jailers were war dancing through the crowd, in search, I suspected, of more satisfying prey. The thick-lipped one, who seemed to be the leader, was mounting the steps of the café, obeying her signs and joining her. I was free.

"The French are crazy," was my Great-Aunt Giuditta's comment when that evening I told her and Aunt Marta what had happened. My great-aunt sat in her cool, high-ceilinged kitchen, in her big, hard armchair, her old face still handsome, still imperious.

"Well, I wondered. The last time I passed *Barba* Miró on the quay he announced that they were arriving in two more days. I asked who they were, and he just kept repeating, 'Crazy, all of them.' He didn't say anything else. I asked several times. He just stroked his mustache the way he does. Now I know. My knees are still shaky."

"Of course, Miró finds most everyone unbalanced." The combination of Giuditta's sudden, almost mischievous smile and the gesture with which she refastened a falling lock of her thick, white hair acted as a crack in her age, exposing the younger self underneath. "You should hear him on the 'returned,' you know those from the village who emigrated to America then came back in retirement. He says none of them returned right in the head. He says their malady has two sources: they've been bitten by the money bug, and they've gone strange from overwork."

We laughed together. "Well, I suppose one thing leads to the other. You lose everything. You find yourself in another place, another world. Money seems like the solution to many things. You want, you need, more and more money. So you overwork. You go . . . *strange.* Anyway, it is true that in North America there's a different attitude. Shops, for example, don't usually close whenever the staff get bored."

Aunt Marta, who lived in Venezia and (like me) was on holiday in Lussino, joined the conversation. "Even in Italy, we aren't that bad. Supply and demand. I think it's just the laziness of the people here. They don't know how to work properly. Of course, with Marxism what can you expect? And three quarters of the time they've sold the few things they have to sell a couple of minutes after opening. If Tito really . . ."

I spoke quickly to avert an argument. "I figured out why they picked on me." (To Aunt Giuditta, in spite of all she had lost, Tito was a hero.)

"Barbarians, communists, addicts . . ." The lines on Marta' face gave her a permanently affronted expression.

"Marta, think. You constantly complain about the difficulties of your life as a chambermaid: dependent on tips, cleaning up the messes of the dirty rich. You complain about how much bread and meat and medicine cost in Venezia. Yet you are so quick to condemn our government here."

"At the last election, I was frightened. They said that if the communists got in they would burn down all the churches."

"They said?" Giuditta shook her head. "What do *they* know? Really . . ."

From my dress pocket, I pulled out a headband, black with green embroidery. "I was wearing this and I suppose . . ."

"What did you expect? Thoughtless one. And with braids yet. You should be more careful. You don't think; you're in this perpetual daze." Marta was clearing off the table, scrubbing the marble with short, sharp motions.

"In Edmonton, headbands are considered too 1960s, but they don't merit a second look. Besides I had a reason for wearing it. It was the first gift given to me by someone I wanted to think about." My aunts thought I had been sent to the island by my parents to recover from a broken heart. Not wanting to explain the actual situation, I gave them portions, snippets of the truth to keep them happy and forestall prying. "Since it encircled my mind, so to speak . . . I thought . . . never mind. It didn't work anyway." Aunt Marta and Aunt Giuditta exchanged meaningful glances. "And now, I can only see it as an affectation. They've ruined it." I stood up, walked across the kitchen and dropped the headband into the garbage. I saw a flash of Daryl sending me one of his quizzical how-could-you looks. Give it a rest, I said to him in my head.

"You see why we're so protective." Aunt Marta grabbed my arm as I crossed back to my chair. "Listen to me. There are dangers here too. Just because it's small . . ."

"Oh, for heaven's sake, Zia." We had argued the previous night. "Not again."

Yesterday afternoon at the beach, I had met two local girls: Clara and Sandra. I was walking along the edge of the water, and they were spread out on towels on the sand. "Teresa," they called, "Teresa Pomoronzola," using the Lanza nickname. I glanced back at Marta, who was half out of her deck chair. She was frowning and gesturing for me to come back. As I hesitated, the two girls jumped up. One was short with dark curls, the other tall, bottle-blond hair and brown skin. Both wore faded, untrendy swimsuits.

"You're the Canadian one," said the shorter one.

"Your mother married the engineer from Bolzano," said the blonde.

"Not Bolzano – Bologna," said the other.

"How on earth? Ah, village hotline."

They introduced themselves. The brunette was Clara, the blonde Sandra. I waved back at Marta and, without a second thought, joined them. I had no trouble understanding them; they spoke to me in Istro-Veneto, the old language of the island that I had heard since birth. Chatting, we walked towards the hut that was the beach bar.

"Let me offer you a coca-cola," said Clara.

"Cigarette?" said Sandra, pulling a slim, sky-blue package labelled Opatija from her bag.

In minutes, we were arrayed on a bench, laughing, drinking coke and smoking. "You must come out with us some evenings," said Clara.

I was feeling slightly nauseated and dizzy from the unfamiliar tobacco after weeks of abstinence. "Umm . . ." I said.

"Away from the old women," said Sandra. "Before you turn into one of them."

They were part of a group that met on the beach in the evening to barbecue over an open fire. Or to party in one of the ruined houses. Later they visited the discos in MaliLosinj. "Dancing?' I said. "Count me in. Definitely." In Edmonton, neither Daryl nor Tony liked to dance, and I was deprived.

The aunts immediately overreacted. They insisted I could not possibly go alone. The clubs did not open until midnight, and how could I walk home from the bigger town in the middle of the night?

"There are no lamps, no illumination on the road between Mali and here. You could meet who knows who in the dark and then what would you do?" Giuditta said. "The island is overrun with foreigners, strangers."

"Germans, Serbs, French," Marta said. "Any one of them could be a rapist or a murderer."

"We don't know them," Aunt Giuditta said. "And at night, when everyone is sleeping, or should be sleeping, at night in the dark . . . well, who knows?"

"I don't intend to go alone," I said. "I'm going with Sandra, Sandra Baricevich. I told you I met her at the Rovenska beach. She isn't from away. So I don't see the problem." (Not mentioning that Clara had told me that she wasn't allowed to the clubs.)

"Oh, that one," Aunt Giuditta said. "Everyone knows about her. If you began to be seen with her, everyone would jump to the wrong conclusions about you."

"I don't give a fig about what people think."

Aunt Giuditta's parchment-white skin managed to turn one shade whiter. "I don't suppose that you do, but, Teresa, you are my niece."

"Not exactly."

"Fine, daughter of my niece. The point is that what you do reflects on me. You are not anonymous here." She was holding herself tall in the armchair. "I do have a position in this town."

I had been angry at both my aunts last night, and now – as Giuditta again reminded me of my responsibilities to the Lanza name and to her, a woman who was respected, looked up to – I was swept up again by a tumultuous wave. I wished I could expose them to the freedom, the casualness, of the undergraduate life I had been leading in Edmonton. If only I could show them my world where drug-taking and premarital sex were taken for granted, then they would see how silly their protectiveness was. "I'm not a little girl," I said. "I'm a woman of the world."

Marta snorted; Giuditta cackled. "A woman of the world, excuse me." One had lived thirty more years than I, the other sixty. From the perspective of those years, they viewed me as naive and ignorant of life. It was not a question of license versus puritanism. My great aunt had achieved her preeminent position as *grande dame* of the island not through her family (respectable enough) nor through her marriage (again a "good" match) but through her judicious choice of lovers. Her husband was a *barba*, a sea captain, a job involving long stretches away from home and later a permanent absence due to that sailor's disease: syphilis. Her lovers were bachelors or widowers and always grateful. All through her middle years she grew richer; her lovers died one by one, always leaving an unexpected legacy. She amassed jewellery, antiques, old masters, houses and pieces of land all over the island. In her old age, as she had gathered, so she lost. "Like vultures they came and picked me clean," she would say of the families of her lovers, of her own relatives and of the communist officials. "Times have been difficult."

Proud, she sat in her black dress and white Venetian lace collar, proud, her wrinkled and veined hands sparkling with rings. I wanted to call her hypocrite, but the gulf was too great.

Besides, when the anger ebbed away, I was left with admiration. She did command respect, and everyone, even the newcomers, bobbed their heads or doffed their caps to her. And this despite her refusing to learn Serbo-Croatian. She spoke in Istro-Veneto or Italian through all the years when both were forbidden. She flaunted her Italianness when Italian ethnics were branded as traitors, when they were imprisoned, exiled or taken to the pits and shot. She must have played and used the rules of her society with such subtlety. Whereas I, in the era of free love, seemed to manage all the wrong moves. How many times last winter had a friend taken me aside to say, "You must decide. It has gone on long enough" or "It's got to be one or the other." I was drowning in disapproval.

Aunt Marta laid out the supper: local goat cheese, fresh rolls, a salad of sliced tomatoes. Aunt Giuditta passed me her lavender handkerchief. I wiped away my stray tears. "Go to the beach," she said. "But no Mali, no discos. And be home at a decent hour . . . Now, if Marino were here. We wouldn't worry with Marino." She took back the handkerchief and tucked it up one of her sleeves. "He'd take you dancing." Difficult for me to imagine since I thought of him as still four years old, still the round-faced, pouting cherub of my memory and the family photograph album. "You were so cute together, you two."

"I remember. He was afraid of the water. I loved to push him in and listen to him scream."

So, after supper, I joined Sandra, Clara and about twenty others on the Rovenska beach. There was a firepit and fish grilling on a makeshift pyramid of stones and a guy with a guitar, a sickle moon, a breeze, and bottles of country red wine. To the majority, who were locals, Clara introduced me as Teresa Pomoronzola or as Signora Lanza's niece, and they shook my hand, welcome, kissed my cheeks, welcome, welcome, and twice hugged me. My identity for the six young men who weren't *Lussignani* was Teresa, *Kanagin,* while they were introduced as from Belgrade or Bosnia or Montenegro. We exchanged nods. Mikki, the guy with the guitar, ran his fingers from back to front through his hair so that it hung in his eyes. He held his guitar out and slightly to the side. He hit three ascending chords.

"Love, love, love," he sang, sounding as if he were a Liverpuddlian. *"All you need is love."*

"He's a Serb," Sandra said. "He's crazy."

"Crazy?"

"Crazy can be good. I like him very much. *Matto dobra*, we say here, *dobra* means good in Croatian."

They all sang along, striking poses, miming microphones. Even I joined in when Mikki started "I Can't Get No Satisfaction."

"And I try and I try," the boys howled. *I can't get no,"* the girls leaned together.

"You like?" said one of the smiling visitors in English

"Dobra," I said, *"dobrissima."* The best – our arms linked, our faces shining in the firelight, singing song after song in ragged harmony.

The next morning, Marta, a couple of her Italian friends, and I hired *Barba* Miró and his boat to take us out past the deserted Hapsburg villas, past the isolated bays where the French were camping, out into the open sea to Iluvik and then Svet Petar. It was on the latter island, San Pietro as it was once called, that I again saw the woman with the long, dark hair, the one who saved me from the war dance in the piazza. San Pietro was a century behind Lussino; the women still carried jars to the well for water, the rosemary grew wild, and the only noise was the sounds of man, his animals and the ever-present cries of the fist-sized crickets. So far from Edmonton where so much of the time I was distanced from the earth, shut in my car, my highrise apartment, even my down parkas and four-lined boots.

Marta and I walked, visited the square, the decaying church, the ruins of an eleventh century Benedictine monastery and some distant cousins. By two in the afternoon, we were sitting at one of the two long tables on a small, vine-trellised terrace jutting out into the bright sea. The sunlight flickered on the white linen tablecloth, the freshly caught scampi in tomato and onion sauce, and the carafes of cold, dry white wine. They arrived in a sailboat, the dark-haired woman and the two men, anchoring casually on the edge of the terrace. The thick-lipped young man jumped off first. He addressed the proprietress in French-accented Italian. "You remember our order?" The dark woman paused on the deck to tie a black sarong over her string bikini, then let herself be helped onto the terrace by the other moustached young man.

They sat at the other table, quite close to me. The proprietress hovered over them in a way she had not with us. The waiter brought the wine and bread immediately, and they had finished a bottle and ordered another before I finished my scampi. They spoke French too quickly for me to understand much of what they were saying. But I could see that the dark lady was clever. She sat in the middle and divided her gaze, smiles, and words equally. She turned to one, then the other, frequently so that neither had a chance to grow bored or think of anything else.

I never had that kind of control. I managed by keeping my men separated, a wall of lies between them. Of course, both Tony and Daryl knew. How could they not in the small university community? But the lies were part of the rules of the relationship. I was supposed to pretend each man was the only one. A friend, who did not understand the rules, told me once that he had challenged Daryl with "she lies to you all the time. You know that." But, to his chagrin, Daryl's only response was a smile. For each one was convinced that eventually he would win. Over those four years there were times we met, the three of us: for long moments at parties, in a class, walking between buildings on campus. I would grow remote with fear, pulling my hand free from whomever was holding on to me, acting as if I had never met either of them before.

Once we smoked dope together. I was inhaling deeply, glad of an excuse to withdraw. They were sitting on either side of me, exchanging polite dope chatter with the others. They looked casual, unconcerned, but I could sense that, underneath, neither of them was relaxed. From one side I could feel Tony's will pushing. From the other, just as strongly, Daryl was demanding. I stared at my black-stockinged thigh, avoiding those eyes that waited for my response, waited for my weakness. Until slowly the stocking began to unravel. As if someone was holding a lighted match to my leg. The skin cracked open, bubbled up black, exposing the pink, wet inner flesh.

When I looked again at the French trio, the men were absorbed in one of those stubborn male exchanges, talking of power politics and Foucault, the significance of which, like so much of that summer, I was not to understand for years. She was silent, looking down, her black satin hair curtaining her face. Finally she lifted her head and looked across the tables straight at me. Her opaque eyes were exhausted.

In the late afternoon Miró dropped us off at Rovenska, claiming the main piazza would be too crowded by that time of day. I was tired from my late night and too much sun and sea. Slowly, I made my way up the path of slippery stones that led to the village. Marta was speculating on how much money one of our cousins on San Pietro received each month from her son in Seattle. "What did you think of the new bathroom? Those tiles. When they still have to haul water . . ." Halfway up the hill, she was out of breath, though still talking, and we paused. A tall man stood at the top, blocking out the setting sun and staring down. Then, as I started walking up again, he started down. When we reached each other, we both stood still, looking. The sky wheeled around me. My legs threatened to buckle.

"But what's happening?" My aunt's voice sounded impossibly far away. I saw only his blue eyes, so bright they seemed neon lit. "Do you know this young man?" I couldn't move, but inwardly I was all motion. "Teresa, this is silly. Are you going to introduce me? Teresa?"

"I have been waiting. I thought I had missed you." He spoke Italian precisely, with a slight Slavic accent.

I finally managed to turn to Marta. "This is Marino, Zia, don't you recognize him?"

"Marino! So many years! You've grown."

"Two metres, at least."

He took my bag, and we fell into step together. "I thought you were in Maribor studying for exams."

"I was." Later, on the way to Mali and a dancing club, he added, "But something drew me home." And still later, as we danced in the garden of the club, once the villa of the mistress of the Archduke Franz Joseph. "I waited and waited and I didn't know what I was waiting for. Then on the wharf I saw a girl with two long red braids, and I knew."

Marino spoke to me not in Istrio-Veneto but in the Italian of books and university courses. Both of us had to think before we spoke, and this gave our words a formal tone, a polish.

That night I replayed those words, replayed each expression on his face, in his eyes, replayed the touch of his hand on the curve of my back, the feel of his tall, broad shouldered body against mine.

In the morning I was in considerable pain. Scattered over my arms and legs were eruptions, perfect white circles blown up with fluid.

"Rest. You are exhausted. No sun. No sea. For a few days. Your skin is too delicate for our island." The doctor was over eighty and nearly blind but still full of the authority of Viennese studies and practice.

"But why hasn't it happened before?"

"The irritation has to build to an intolerable point. Then your body reacts." She burst the balloons with a razor, sprinkled the skin with antibiotic powder and wrapped my arms and legs in bandages.

For the next five days, I was mostly confined to Aunt Giuditta's walled garden. I sat on an old armchair in the shade of the fig tree, my feet on an embroidered stool. Each day Marino would lay on my lap a new gift: a plate of sweet cakes, a bouquet of wild flowers, a record of local love songs, a book of poems. We talked of that summer we had played together as children. I remembered his fear of water and my fearlessness. He remembered my tears and a straw boater I wore everywhere. He produced a picture of both of us in a canoe. He was paddling. He had another picture of him kissing me on the cheek. "You smelt of flowers," he said. "And you still do."

One afternoon, Clara came. "Fancy meeting you here," she said to Marino with a smug smile. And after he left, she laughed and put her hand on mine. "So our golden boy is human after all." She explained that Sandra had not come, because she had always had a crush on Marino. "She thinks it's damn unfair. But he always held himself a bit above the rest of us. I wasn't surprised."

"How did you know? We've only gone out once."

Clara shook her curly head. "In the village, we know everything."

I did not tell Marino what she had said. I sensed he would not be pleased that we were the subject of gossip. Besides, we had so much else to say to each other. We talked for hours and hours. We talked of growing up in Canada and Yugoslavia, of our favourite books, of religion and Marxism and the sexual revolution. "In everything we are the same," Marino would say. I would agree, although it was obvious how very different we were. I would agree, because it was an easy way of expressing our intense kinship, our instant attraction.

He spoke of the problems for him of going to university in Slovenia. "I have to learn a different language. And then I am not at home as I would have been in Zagreb." In secondary school, he had begun training to be a sea captain at the Academy in Malilosinj. When he realized that that path was not for him – I could have told you that, I said – he was not able to get into the university he wanted.

"They hate us," he said. "The Slovenians hate the Croatians. You can't imagine, coming from Canada as you do, how difficult it can be for me."

For the first time, I felt a twinge of irritation. I was sure Marino was over-dramatizing the situation. "I can imagine. Canada is not paradise. We have our regional problems. After all, we have Quebec. Many of its citizens want to separate from Canada. We have had our acts of terrorism: bombs, kidnappings."

"In Yugoslavia, we are divided from top to bottom, Slovenians, Croats, Serbs, Moslems, Montenegrans: each one hates the other. After Tito dies," he paused, "it is going to be chaos."

I was sceptical though thrilled by the seriousness of his tone. Conscious that my Aunt periodically checked on us from her window and that other curious faces stared down from the surrounding houses, I focussed on his large, strong hands, his solid wrists, the golden hairs on his brown arms.

I had never known such desire before. This, I thought as I sat in my Aunt's garden, this is beyond compare.

"What are your intentions for that young man?" Aunt

Giuditta asked when I announced that, bandages removed, my first expedition would be a walk with Marino to the semi-ruined Austrian promenade.

"I thought you asked the man that."

"I don't need to ask Marino anything. I can recognize courtship when I see it." She refastened her hair, her still firm chin thrust farther out than usual.

"Oh Zia, these days . . ." I was absentmindedly fiddling with my own hair, weaving purple flowers from the latest bouquet into my braids.

"In my day, of course, it was different. More substantial. More hothouse flowers and diamond earrings. But what can you expect now? I remember one colonel from Vienna; we met at a ball at that villa up . . ."

"I hope you don't intend to go out like that." This came from Marta who set before me my morning coffee in a delicate china cup decorated with the black Hapsburg eagle. Her sallow face more pursed than usual, she turned to Giuditta. "She's always sticking flowers in her hair or wearing some odd thing. Then she comes home complaining about how they acted in the piazza. She gives no thought to . . ."

"And if he was courting me . . . what would be wrong . . . we've been . . ."

". . . What people will think . . ."

Giuditta's exclamation "Marta" and my "Zia" were simultaneous. Giuditta pulled herself up to full height. "Will you stop fussing. Sit down and keep quiet. How many times have I told you to let me handle these things? As I was saying about the colonel, he began with sweet cakes too . . ."

"And I asked what would be wrong if he was courting me?"

Marta dropped noisily into a hard, wooden chair in the corner. "His mother came to talk to us."

"She was visiting me to see how I was," I said.

"She's very worried."

"Why? Oh Zia, you know what it's like with mothers when they have one son. She has to let go sometime."

Giuditta shook her head. "She says he's supposed to be at the university studying for his final exams."

"He has been studying."

"But how well is he concentrating? This is important. To the whole village. He's the first boy to go to university in years . . . You don't know what it was like here after everyone left. A deserted village. Then people came from the mainland, Serbs, Dalmatians. Slowly, so slowly, Velilosinj came to life again. So it matters. We've had a few lawyers, one or two doctors, certainly, but a scientist! And Marino is Marino. First of all, he is my heir, the little that I have left. And he is the last of the Lanzas, the last of the Stuperichs. The last still here. Everyone has an interest in his success."

"And I?"

"You are a tourist."

"But you're always saying I can't act like an outsider."

"True, because you aren't. You're not one of the anonymous hordes, camping in the hills and sunning nude in the bays. No. But this is just a vacation for you. You will leave. Eventually perhaps you will return for your old aunt and for more sea and sun. But for Marino it is more serious. No, wait, listen to what I am saying. He cannot go and then return."

"What do you mean?" I felt a tremor of anxiety.

"It is not allowed. If he leaves, it will be considered a political decision. Like crossing the Berlin Wall. There can be no coming back."

"You're blowing everything out of proportion." (Thinking that everyone in this place had a tendency to overdramatize.)

"I am trying to teach you proportion."

We grew more devious. We told Aunt Giuditta we were spending the evening with the group, and we did begin with them on the beach or in a café, but when we told them we were going home, our time began. In the wild abandoned garden of a hospital, once a villa. Beneath a flowering magnolia. Skinny dipping in the phosphorescent bay. Each time, beneath a sky of stars.

Marino knew my dark lady. "Journalist. She has been here several summers. Usually she arrives with one; then he leaves on the hydrofoil. On the foil's return, the other one arrives. Amazing timing."

"Sounds familiar," I mumbled in English.

"This is the first time I have seen her with both."

The sea of the island, beneath the superficial brightness, is glass clear, both exposing marine secrets and creating illusions of shallowness. Every second day Marino transported fresh water and food in his uncle's motorboat to where most of the French were camping. I sat in the stern, protected by caftan and sun hat and entranced by the clarity of the depths and my sea-eyed boatsman.

At the bay I usually stayed in the boat. I was still nervous of the French group. Marino, instead, seemed at ease with the tanned throng, exchanging witticisms in French. We were just about to start back, when the thick-lipped young man appeared on the edge of the clearing. He wound his way through the tents, through all the people on the beach. "Will you give me a ride to the village?"

The dark lady was a couple of minutes behind him. Marino was pulling the string to the engine when I saw her running, obviously trying to catch up. She hailed us from the edge of the pier, the gold bangles clattering down her brown arm.

"This is getting crowded," Marino muttered. The young

man stared at the horizon, his lips drawn up in a pout. She settled beside him, opposite me, murmuring to him in a low voice. She was desperate to dissipate his anger. Tentatively she stroked his arm, laid her head on his shoulder, offered smiles to his averted face. Her voice, above the motor, was childlike, cute. My stomach twisted. Gradually he turned to her, softening under her caresses. I looked away.

How many times? Especially after one of those accidental meetings or other such rule infractions. Except for me the scene was not set in a boat or on a blue-blue sea but in a car with windows so thickly iced over that I had no idea where we were. I would talk and talk. He would stare intently out the small, scraped patch of window. And I would feel more and more enveloped by the cold and white. Never again.

"I don't understand," was Marino's comment when I tried to explain it.

"She was humiliating herself. I felt humiliated watching her."

"I don't see why. After all we can presume he had a reason to be angry. He was the humiliated one. She should choose and such situations would not arise."

"Choose. It's not so easy. It is two halves of a circle."

"Inside her heart, she must prefer . . ."

I stopped him with a kiss. And I drank him up, clear, bright and blue.

Marino returned to the mainland to take his exams. I would be leaving soon for London and the charter back to Edmonton. We had grown tense from the lack of time.

I imagined two possible futures. In the first, without any pressure on my part, Marino joined me in Edmonton. One day, out of the blue, he would phone and say: "It's done. I am coming." And then, he would be there at the airport. He would be by my side. Darryl, Tony, all my friends would be surprised, even shocked. "He's the one," I would announce, "my better half." Marino and I would have to move, say to Toronto, so that we could both find fulfilling and high paying work. But the core of the fantasy was the two of us together and happy in Canada.

The other possibility was harder to envision. Who would I have been if my mother never left Lussino? If I had been born and raised there? I saw myself more confident, more courageous: a T.V. newscaster in Trieste, a reporter in Zagreb. We would be dissidents, of course, intellectuals with a city apartment and a summer house on the island. The house Giuditta used to own – why not – on the promontory overlooking the sea, the house with spacious rooms, leatherbound books, oriental carpets, and large Chinese vases.

"It would be tough," I told Marino, "learning another alphabet, as well as another language." I heard my mother's voice. *You have no idea.*

"It can be done. Some concentrated study. And you would find work, teaching English say."

"Couldn't you come to visit me? Just a visit?"

"It is not so easy," Marino said.

You have no idea.

I pushed away the thought of my mother and the nostalgia that hung like a stone around her neck. "That's it exactly. In Canada, things are easy. We're free. You could have a good future there."

Marino placed a kiss in the centre of my palm. "I don't know. There is my mother."

But the next evening he said: "A new country, a new freedom, a real future and you. *Lusinga, lusinga.*"

After Marino left for his exams, as I waited for his return, the word *lusinga* hissed in my ear, lay on my lips, crouched at the root of my tongue and imprinted on my eyelids. I was sure

I knew the meaning of *lusingare* he intended. Canada enticed him. I enchanted and seduced him.

Aunt Marta and I were crossing the piazza on our return from the post office when I sparked off French hilarity again. I was engrossed in a letter from Tony. I could feel his will rising from the carefully printed words. "No matter what you say, if you were here and I could put my head on your little round belly . . ." It was the thick-lipped one again. He pulled off my large sun hat and perched it at an angle on his dark curls. Immediately a tiny blonde girl stretched up and claimed the hat. I looked over at the woman who was sitting, as I knew she would be, on the terrace. But she was listening to the other one, her face in her hands, and she paid no attention. I couldn't wait until they stopped. The hat was being passed hand to hand. I grabbed my aunt, who was yelling indignantly, and pulled her away.

"Let them have it."

Aunt Giuditta was waiting for us at her door. "What have you done to that poor boy?"

"Who? Marino? He isn't even here."

"Oh, he's here. Stopped in a while ago looking for you. He travelled all night to get back. He nearly fainted on the kitchen floor. He hadn't eaten anything. I ordered him home."

"I must go."

"No. He has to rest. After all, he just wrote those exams. Then the trip. What his mother said when she saw him I do not know. All white he was: pale. And dirty."

"O.K. I'll wait a bit."

"You better sit down and listen to Zia Giuditta," Marta ordered, shoving me towards a chair.

Giuditta sat in a composed manner, her beringed hands crossed, her chin in the air. "This is becoming more and more serious... Now listen to me, child; you must think of Marino's mother. He is an only child, and she is widowed."

"I know that."

"But do you realize her position if he left the country? Especially before he did his military service?"

You have no idea, my mother said. *Exile*.

"You two have been acting as if you're out of your heads," Marta commented from her usual position at the sink.

"I understand." Giuditta's faded eyes met mine. "I do. But Marta's right. You must be rational about this. You must think."

I controlled myself for a couple of hours. But then I was off down the slippery path to Rovenska. Not wanting to deal with his mother, I didn't go to the door but stood under the balcony of his room and called up. He had brought me a carved wooden bird from Rijeka. "A nightingale to remember me and the island."

"I won't need a reminder," I said. So you have made up your mind, I thought.

"Some say that the name Lussino came from *usignuolo*, the nightingale."

We walked to the old promenade, he eagerly telling me of his odyssey – his hitchhiking and walk cross country. "Through these woods. Miles and miles. There were enormous cobwebs stretched out across the path in some places." But only vaguely did I take in what he was saying. His physical presence and the beating waves distracted me. Usually the promenade was silent and dark, but that night loud laughter and screeching interrupted us. Looking out through the stone arch that had once been a window, we saw a group of people in evening dress. From the way their lamps weaved about, we guessed they were drunk.

"I forgot," Marino whispered in my ear. "Today's Bastille

Day." One of the women, standing on the edge of a rock, her black beaded dress glittering in the moonlight, stretched, arched and dove into the sea. Laughing, a few of the others threw themselves in.

"They're crazy. The sea's rough, lots of whitecaps."

"Crazy. Nothing deters them. Look," he pointed out to sea. "There's a sailboat out there."

"My trio, no doubt. Drunk like the rest on *slivovic*."

"How do you know?"

"I can imagine."

The bottle being passed, their wills pushing, pushing for her weakness. Until not the strongest, who knew how to wait, but the most desperate took her down below to force pleasure upon her. To prove that he could, under the nose of the other. To plant, in revenge, yet another seed of humiliation.

Marino wanted to go into the hills to one of the abandoned houses, in an attempt to escape the ever increasing wind, but I wouldn't leave the sea. Lightning ripped the horizon, illuminating the pounding waves and his serious face. We wedged ourselves into a ledge on the cliff bordering the sea path. "I saw your face before me the whole time I was away." I answered with kisses lit by the approaching storm.

Marino was with me and in me. But it was not enough. I wanted more and more, an end of longing, a sense of arrival, a sailing home. I held him, and he was unholdable, a wind, a wave. We were together yet already the yearning was choking me.

But she rebelled, my dark lady. It was the patient one who went below, and she and the thick-lipped one remained above, screaming back and forth at each other as they tried to turn the boat towards land. Her anger, so suddenly loosened, beat against her conscious mind. He was bent, adjusting the sheet lines to reduce the sails while she stood at the tiller steering. Her anger, like the waves battering the rocks. "More to the right," he lifted his head to deliver the order. Without thought, her hand pulled left.

The boom swung across, catching him as he began to straighten. She watched him fall. She screamed for help. The sea engulfed so quickly. She screamed to the other below.

Back in Edmonton, in one of my mother's history books, I read that some thought that the name Lussino came from *lusinga*, to enchant, for that was what the island did: enchant each and every one. But when I looked up *lusinga* in Zingarelli's Italian dictionary it was defined as not only to enchant, but also to delude, to flatter, to deceive, from the German word *lausinga*, a lie. My return to the island did help me to escape what I needed to escape. It served. Yet, when I remember Lussino, I feel both enchanted and deceived.

The day after the storm, the body was sighted, and Marino was called to retrieve it. I wanted to go with him. "I'll sit quietly in the boat. I just want to watch you dive." But he refused. I sat on the rock from where the woman in the evening dress had jumped and watched Marino's boat until it was just a black dot on the bright sea.

Multiculturalism

I

When her friends questioned Margaret on the wisdom of her dating an alleged Mafioso, she would laugh and say, "I'm an Italiophile; I love all things Italian." And, indeed, it was because she had been to Italy and studied Italian that she caught the attention of Salvatore Peldioca (known affectionately as Sonny – the Goose.)

On Saturdays, she worked in the shop of the Royal Ontario Museum, and it was there that she met Sonny. He was questioning the other clerk about the relative merits of two paintings in the current megashow, so he could decide which reproduction to buy. Margaret took a long look at his classically proportioned face and body, then another look at his thick dark curls, and on a purely aesthetic impulse (as she explained to a friend later), she left her post at the cash register.

The other girl, impelled by some impulse of her own, was smiling a winsome smile as she talked of personal taste. Margaret positioned herself by his elbow. "I would say that it's a question of the linear versus the painterly," she said in Italian. He turned to her, his eyes alive with interest. He wanted to know how she knew Italian and, then, how long she had been in Italy and where and why she decided to study art. And those words she used? Were they descriptive or judgmental? What exactly did they mean – linear? painterly? In her break, they had coffee in the museum café, but though she stretched fifteen minutes into twenty-five, there was only enough time to begin to explain. He went back into the museum until she finished work, so that he could drive her home and they could talk. The romance had begun.

"You're not serious?" her friends said when she described Sonny: his looks, his brightness, his white Cadillac with red leather upholstery and, according to one of her ex-classmates in Italian 425 who saw them having lunch together at the university cafeteria, his murky reputation.

"Serious? Maggie and the loanshark? Or is it just loan collector? I only have gossip to go on, you know. Serious? Of course not."

And that was the point, she admitted to herself. She had always been too serious, too careful. Her mother had often accused her, though usually she presented the accusations as praise, insisting that Margaret was never any trouble, that she had been born tidy, polite and responsible. Solemn Sis, her older brother would call her if she tried to argue the necessity of recycling or the dangers of overdevelopment to our national parks or any of the other thousand and one issues she was passionate about. "If you never risk, you never win," her mother warned her when, as a junior, she decided to switch from fine arts to art history because it seemed safer and more settled. "Your father," her mother said, "taught me that. He was a brave man."

"I know," Margaret said, "and a talented one. But I haven't inherited either attribute."

Margaret was titillated by her daring and by how out of character she was acting. Not that she didn't soon impose limitations on her romance with Sonny. The first time he invited her out to dinner, she made her face as mournful as possible. "My family," she told Sonny in her most demure tones, "does not let me go out in the evening." She had not observed all those Italian-Canadian girls from Woodbridge in her Italian classes for nothing. She knew that despite the masses of hair, the flashy earrings, the elaborate make up and the miniskirts, many of them lived restricted lives. She knew that while an Italian in Italy would laugh in disbelief, an Italian-Canadian might accept her excuse.

"I understand." Sonny said. "As it happens, much of my work is at night. My days are often free."

They quickly established a routine, a satisfying routine. She worked at home for a couple of hours in the morning. Sonny would arrive in his Cadillac about eleven. They would take a drive and often end up at the racetrack for lunch. Sonny would place his bets and confer with a colleague or two. Margaret would wait for him in the restaurant, content for awhile with the view of the track and her most recent thoughts on Giotto's *Vision of Joachim*. When he rejoined her, he would order what was for those pre-gourmet Toronto days a princely lunch: snails, paté or onion soup, a bottle of beaujolais, filet mignon or lobster, caesar or green salad. They would alternately converse and cheer on Sonny's horses.

He was eager to hear her speak of Italy; he had left when he was ten years old and never been back. She complied with mini lessons in Italian Civilization. "What we need is some slides," she would joke, and she did take to bringing postcards. Sonny was particularly drawn to the Renaissance, and though it was not her favourite period, she dwelt at length on Michelangelo and Da Vinci, the Borgias and the Gonzagas, the Pope and Galileo. They would drink several cups of coffee. He would insist, despite her protestations, on feeding her spoonfuls of his chocolate mousse in celebration.

"Your horses," she pointed out to him, "win surprisingly often. I could get fat."

"They win," he said, "cause you bring me luck."

"So that's what I am to you," she said. "A charm."

"Baby, you're the best," he said.

He would drop her off in mid-afternoon at the Robarts library. Relaxed, she would work hard on her thesis until late into the evening. It was an ordered and fruitful time for her. She finished the first draft of her thesis in three months rather than the six her supervisor expected. And Sonny was *her* special charm. His exaggerated, loose-hipped walk, his lowered-eyelid, slow burning stare, the New Yorkish twang in his voice and even the way he called her Baby or Sweetheart and promised her the stars, all was as enticing to her, as fixed and as foreign as Giotto's frescoes.

How she felt when he touched her was equally enticing, but not foreign; no, it erupted from within, and not fixed, unfortunately, not at all fixed. With racing season over, they changed restaurants. They spent more time in the Cadillac: parked. "Going native," Sonny joked. "At this rate we'll start a forest fire."

Margaret did not smile. If he ever went further, say if he ever jokingly referred to her as squaw, it would be the end. But he never crossed that line. She hadn't intended to tell him of her background; in her teens and early twenties it seemed to have only a private significance. But it had slipped out. Sonny had taken her to a soccer game one Sunday afternoon and introduced her to several old high school friends. One in particular, a stocky, big-nosed youth, had seemed startled by Margaret. He hadn't followed the banter but stared fixedly at her. When he finally did speak, he told a Wop joke. Then he had laughed loudly, his eyes still on Margaret, while the others groaned theatrically. Another of the group, one with a long, morose face, began with the usual propaganda: "We're all immigrants here . . ."

"Speak for yourselves," she'd interrupted. "I'm a Canadian, period. No hyphen." Later, when Sonny drove her home, she had explained that her mother's family had arrived almost two hundred years before and that her father was a full-blooded Cree. "He was adopted when he was three."

Eventually Margaret invited Sonny home for dinner, partly to forestall an introduction to his family and partly to allay his suspicions that she was amusing herself with him, "playing with danger."

"Are you telling me you're dangerous?" she asked.

"I'm warning you I'm serious," he said.

And he turned up that Sunday evening in a serious blue suit, his hair slicked back, and with two dozen roses. "How wonderful," her mother said at least three times. For the occasion, Jean was wearing a hand-loomed caftan and had set the table with irregular-shaped pottery. She offered sherry in earthenware cups but, before Sonny could take a sip, she lay her hand on his arm. "You must see the paintings." She held onto him as she guided him through the rooms. "Now, look at this. Stunning. Don't you agree? Simply stunning. Even after all these years, I find it . . ." She opened her free hand, fingers splayed, expressing how words failed her.

Sonny's face remained closed before the abstract in black, brown and red. He cleared his throat in a sound that approximated agreement. "This was one of his earlier works," Margaret said. "He was still being influenced by the New York school, I mean, the Abstract Expressionists. I mean, he was always interested in colour field painting but later . . ."

"No need to get technical, dear. My Joseph was an original. He copied no one." She steered Sonny towards the stairwell. "He came to himself and his subject late." They paused half way up the stairs to consider the large canvas hanging at the top. "Now this is *Coyote Shops at Eaton's*, the only one of his famous Coyote series that we still own."

Sonny stared at the swirl of colours that was both the eye of energy and the mythological figure and said, "Wow!"

"I know," Margaret piped up from her spot behind her mother on the stairs. "That's the standard reaction."

Jean edged past Sonny. "Come. You must see this next one." She led down the hall to her room. "He called it: *You Can't Roller Skate in a Buffalo Herd*. Wonderful, isn't it? You see, when he began to explore the native ways, to open himself to the spirits . . ."

"Mother, don't start with that stuff," Margaret said.

"To burn with the vision." The words poured from her mouth, but Jean's face was fixed in a polite smile and a bemused expression. "Well, he was a great man with a great talent."

"He burned us and himself," Margaret muttered to herself not for the first time.

Jean kept on smiling and delivering her monologue: " . . . Twisting, turning, extending the old myths . . ."

Sonny had not heard what Margaret had said; his head was inclined towards her mother, but he did turn and send her a long look. Then he said, "I like the colours."

"I told you Dad always had good colour sense."

"Colour sense! That hardly . . ." Jean tried to interrupt her daughter.

"And if you notice the clarity and the sharpness of his line, yes, in the symbolical figures, you'll see the connection with . . ."

"I thought I was giving the tour, Maggie. Look, be a dear and check on the roast. Give Salvatore and me some time to get acquainted. Please?"

Half an hour passed before Jean and Sonny rejoined Margaret, her brother Colin, and the sherry. "He's very charming," the mother said loudly to the daughter.

Sonny spoke softly, almost whispering in her ear. "I'm

surprised you haven't told me more about your father." Jean was busy speaking to Colin. "You seem almost embarrassed."

"Oh well, Mother has her spiel. It seems simple now, and wonderful. But it wasn't then, when I was little. It was confusing." For Margaret remembered too vividly her father's long absences and her mother's tears. And Colin had told her how their father had been successful before he "came to his subject." Typically, Colin had saved in a scrapbook all the angry reviews of the paintings their father was later to be famous for. Joseph was attacked for not being Indian enough, for disrespect, impurity and disrupting the tradition. He was also attacked for limiting, ghettoising and trivializing his art by the use of so-called native content.

Colin's favourite phrase was "forewarned means forearmed." He did not need to exaggerate much to play the role of the protective older brother who would not allow his sister to date after dark. Through dinner, he watched Sonny. He asked the expected questions. He did accept Sonny's answers as to his interests, intentions and career prospects with a neutral face. He did say, "Oh, really?" when Sonny said he was in the money market. But he smiled amicably when Sonny spoke of his "dreams of diversification."

Over dessert, a tough crusted apple pie, Sonny requested permission to see Margaret in the evening. Jean and Colin had been briefed. Jean flashed her best fake smile. Colin said they were an old-fashioned family but now that they knew Sonny a little perhaps something – something reasonable – could be worked out.

Sonny was not fooled. "They didn't like me," he said as Maggie walked him to his car.

"I thought Mum was enthusiastic."

"She was. But not about me."

"Come on. She couldn't have been more polite."

"Probably not."

"They're slow to warm up to anyone. I told you."

"I should have taken off my pinkie ring." He lifted his hand to rub his nose. The light from the streetlight bounced impressively off the diamond. His smile was rueful and hers matched.

She agreed with her mother and brother, who expressed their opinion repeatedly in the next few days, that she had to break it off, that fun was fun, charming was charming, but it was not fair or wise to continue. Sonny's intentions, as he coaxed her yet again into the backseat, as flesh and leather groaned one more time, were clear. He wanted a wife.

"I haven't been entirely honest with you," she told him. "I have a fiancé." She had made mention of Massimo several times; now she elaborated. They had met in Padova at the Arena Chapel itself. Massimo was also interested in art, finishing a degree in architecture. In fact, she had been at the chapel searching for a thesis topic, and he had been there doing research for an article. They had a lot in common, amazingly so, and the long separation had confirmed it. (Massimo indeed had begun to write more frequently and romantically but the appellation fiancé was stretching things a bit.)

"You think he's serious, this guy?" Sonny said. "This Eyetalian? The Venetian Count and the *tourista*. Tell me another one." But he also said, "Don't worry. I get it. I got it a long time ago."

II

Ironically, six months later Maggie and Massimo were married – twice. First, in Toronto at Knox United in a service which featured poems by Petrarch and Shakespeare and personally written vows and was followed by champagne punch, munchies and cake in her uncle's garden. Then, in Venice in *la Chiesa dei Gesuiti*, a more traditional rite, after which they were borne away in a gondola to a seven-course dinner on Torcello.

Jean and Colin attended both ceremonies. They had given Maggie a trip to Italy supposedly as a graduation present but actually to ensure that she was finished with Sonny. They hadn't expected the result but were pleased. Massimo was the right kind of Italian: from an old, austere and, as Jean said, tasteful family.

And, at first, through Massimo, the Italy that Maggie loved was hers – at her window, at her doorstep, in the long dark corridors of the family apartment. The daily reminders of what man has been and made – in the eighteenth-century chandelier, in the seventeenth-century silverware, in the anonymous Renaissance painting that hung on their bedroom wall. Even the shape of Massimo's head, the set of his face, his sloe eyes carried an insistent echo of history. At home, Jean revered her husband's paintings, the experts respected them and the average man had never heard of him. In Venice, everyone was a connoisseur; there was a casual familiarity with beauty that manifests itself in the tying of a scarf or the subtle combinations of flavours in a meal.

At first. And at last, too, but in between, another Italy asserted itself, where care and carelessness were doled out in mistaken proportions, where the phrases *la bella figura* and *arrangiarsi* were too apt and where her mother-in-law criticized her hair and clothes and manner with guests.

They did not stay in Venice. They gypsied back and forth, in search of a proper home and proper work. In Canada, Margaret taught art history as an itinerant worker, a course here, a course there, and Massimo worked as a sales representative for various Italian firms. In Italy, they waited for connections and possibilities to bear fruit: picking up cash by guiding a tour or doing a review, following leads for the ever-elusive apartment in Venice. Margaret felt awkward and obtrusive living in her in-laws' apartment, but Massimo refused to consider the mainland an alternative.

Eventually a job worthy of Massimo's talents did turn up – in Edmonton. And the day after they arrived, Margaret was hired to manage an Indian and Eskimo art gallery. She was hired because she was her father's daughter, which embarrassed her for the first few months. Her feeling of fraudulence gradually faded as she began to read, to study and, most important, to look at native art. And once familiar, she was able again to trust her aesthetic instincts.

Massimo was hired because he was Italian, as was Lo Schiavo, the developer who hired him saying, "I need someone who can understand me." Lo Schiavo had left Italy only two years before, he said, because of the terrorism: "no one is safe, no one." He had an oversized head, a grey beard and thick voice, all of which lent him an authoritative air. "Government? Italy has no government," he would pronounce, along with all the other usual clichés about the country he had left. He alternated these with clichés of what was wrong with the country he had adopted. "No style," he would say, "none. No drive and . . ." He was remedying matters with the splendour of his projects: condominiums in Vancouver, a shopping centre in Saskatoon, high rises in Edmonton – all flush with marble and brass.

"All totally alien to this place," Margaret complained.

Massimo shrugged in a way that telegraphed his family's antiquity. "New money, new Neapolitan money yet. What can you expect? I do find him and his ideas rather amusing."

"Ideas! He has no ideas. But he thinks that he knows everything and that if we all listened to him . . ."

"Come on. He's refreshing after all the wishy-washy Canadians."

"Wishy-washy? Polite! We don't broadcast our opinions at the loudest frequency."

"So I notice."

"But even you –"

"Meaning?"

"Even a foreigner must see that thing you're working on is wrong for Edmonton," Margaret said.

"Clashes with the dominant style?" Massimo laughed.

Many arguments and two years later, they discovered Lo Schiavo was merely a front. The real owner of the company Massimo worked for was a *Signore Malvio*, a Milanese banker.

"How odd," said Margaret.

"Not at all," said Massimo. "Probably something to do with taxes." And again he shrugged.

Odder still, the banker owned a ranch west of Edmonton and, without ever having met Massimo, he had invited them out for the day.

She did not want to go. She was eight months pregnant and spent her weekends resting, but Massimo stressed the man's importance: his picture was often in *L'Espresso*. Such an opportunity and no one else from the firm was invited.

Lo Schiavo was at the cement bunker ranch house, as well as two cabinet ministers, the owner of a beloved sports team, a corporate president and respective wives. One look at those faces familiar from newspapers and T.V. and Margaret felt lightheaded, then unaccountably irritated. Massimo plunged into the living room the size of their house with all the self-promoting instincts and the confidence of a Venetian *gentiluomo*. Crossing over to the central fireplace, a sort of stone firepit with a huge iron hood, he smiled slightly and nodded in response to inquiring glances, as if he were also a celebrity.

Upon reaching the little group of Lo Schiavo, his wife and one of the cabinet ministers, he shook hands all around. Margaret had not taken a step, and he was in mid chat.

A short, pale man with a tidy mustache appeared at her elbow. "But this is dreadful. Didn't my butler . . .? Come, you must sit down." His style, unlike that of his front man, was discreet, his voice soft. "How wonderful that you could come. I was hoping." His flowery courtesy left her feeling even more embarrassed. "I particularly wanted to talk to you," he said, switching into Italian. "I'm rather well-known as a collector, you know. And you can help me," he added before passing her along to his stone-faced wife.

The gathering, after drinks and through a buffet lunch, divided by gender. Across the room, the men spilled a river of words. The women's conversation had no such flow. Margaret concentrated on the view through the floor to ceiling windows. Talk of drycleaners, wash cycles, housekeepers and stains swirled about her head. Now and then one of the women would ask her a question about her pregnancy or tell a story about her own experience in a way that demanded an answer. Margaret would reluctantly focus on whichever blonde-streaked wife was speaking. Why did all of these women have variations of the same great mane hairdo? And why did they harp on about either cleanliness or blood?

"No," Margaret said, "I've never had a miscarriage." And later: "Oh dear, how awful" to a tale of birth trauma and consequent retardation.

She was relieved from expressing more inanities when, at coffee, Mr. Malvio took the just vacated place beside her on the sofa. He questioned her about her training and her work at the gallery. He sat sideways, his arm hooked over the back of the sofa, his hand an inch away from her shoulder. This position gave the impression that he was totally intent on their conversation, but Margaret suspected that the banker was using it to prevent himself from sinking, as she had, too deeply into the cushions.

He asked what to look for in Eskimo sculpture. He already had a few antique pieces of what he called native memorabilia, some Dorset, some Thule, that he had acquired from a German Count, and he had decided he would like an important collection. "There is much demand for the pieces by the top sculptors, true?"

"Oh, they sell. They're the only sculptures in this country that do sell." She was beginning to wish he would move on. She was both sleepy and queasy from the too rich lunch.

"We're all bored with the latest jokes from the post-post-post-crowd. Our society, my dear lady, is too sophisticated. We need the savage innocence . . ."

"The sense of unity and harmony," offered Lo Schiavo, who had taken the chair opposite and was watching them with a self-satisfied air. Malvio did not even turn his head. "The primal vitality to cleanse our satiated . . ."

There was no way that she could quickly and gracefully get up from the marshmallow sofa. She was trapped by the size of her belly. Lo Schiavo was leaning forward, physically trying to impose himself. As soon as Malvio paused to search for a word, he jumped in. "To remind us of the wholeness of life."

She did not intend to snap but did. "You mean the wholeness of lifestyle." Without thinking, she had switched to English.

"Pardon?" The two men exchanged a look – what is this little Canadian talking about?

"Lifestyle. This," she waved her hand at the room, the fireplace and the large canvases so carefully hung. "Testament to your taste and your worth. You don't have to give me the whole line."

"The whole line? I'm not familiar with this expression." Malvio was looking amused. "But I am most sincere and most serious about this. I have deep feelings for primitive art."

"Let's get real." This phrase brought another show of mystification. "Right out that window, this land borders the Duffield reserve. Have you any idea of the suicide rate among your neighbours? Primal vitality? Sure, check out the braves as they lay themselves down on the railroad tracks. Innocence . . ."

"Margaret." Massimo was standing behind the sofa, his hand clamped down on her shoulder.

She pinched the back of his hand, "Let go." She turned back to the banker but he had made his escape. He and his wife were offering the guests a choice of afternoon activities: riding, hiking or pool.

"Have you gone crazy?" Massimo whispered. "Such rudeness. And to a man who could do so much for me. For you."

Their argument lasted all the way back to the city. She didn't know what excuse Massimo gave. Pregnancy was handy for quick exits. Actually, she was feeling queasier and queasier. She asked Massimo to be careful on the curves and potholes. He ignored her. "It's what you do every day," he said. "Now, all of a sudden, it's wrong?" he said. "Hypocrite."

She explained she had been uneasy for some time, processing planeload after planeload of Eskimo art, and that the banker's foolishness had made her see why. He saw only that she had deliberately sabotaged him and his career. She tried again. Her new knowledge was intuitive and she managed words and phrases but with little coherence. "Ghetto," she said, "tourist art," she said. "Their cultural expression, their essence, becomes an object, devoid of meaning, mere decoration," she said.

He responded by ridiculing her naivety, earnestness and lack of savvy. Her flaws were Canadian flaws and demonstrated why he would never feel at home here. His problems in Canada were her fault. Besides, she was cold, conforming, egotistical, provincial and superior. Likewise, she held him responsible for and as an example of Italy's down side: he was self-indulgent, disorganized, egotistical, provincial and superior. "Theorize all you want," Massimo said. "You can't face the fact your father died on a bender."

When she threw up lunch, she felt as if she was throwing up the marriage. The meal had been exquisite: Buffalo milk cheese, miniature quail, triple cream and strawberries of the forest, delicacies rare in the West. But the effect was cloying, the aftertaste gall.

Despite Massimo's prediction, Margaret's outburst did not harm his prospects. He was given more work, more money, and soon after Alex was born, several trips to Italy. In turn, she quit her job and, when Alex napped, began doing watercolour landscapes. She showed these to no one: they felt as personal as doodles.

Alex was often ill, the pediatrician blamed allergies, and in his second year pneumonia followed chicken pox. Margaret was already worn out from her own bout with bronchitis. Massimo was no help; he seemed to view his family's frailties as personal insults. (Besides, he insisted he didn't believe in allergies. "In Italy, no one has allergies," he'd say. "Never heard of them.") Margaret took Alex home to Toronto for a restorative visit and her usual week with her mother stretched into three months. During the last few days, at the premiere party after a play, she ran into Sonny. She was turning away from the buffet table, trying to manage a plate of Dim Sum (it was a play about Chinese immigrants), a cup of tea and her purse when her arm struck his. They started, laughed and hugged. Sonny pointed to his wife across the room. "Ah, yes," Margaret said, "I heard you were married about a week after we parted company."

"Not a week," he said. "But I told you I was serious," he said. And after the necessary exchange on how well each of them looked: "Where's the count?"

She described his job, the company and, for some reason, even the banker. Sonny did not seem surprised at the amount of detail she gave. "So he stays on his toes?" he asked, holding her glance in a way she thought was significant. "Watches the Eyeties?" Stock phrases or a warning? She wasn't sure. He moved on to praise his twin girls and the surprising joys of fatherhood; she responded with a picture of Alex.

"You're right," she said, staring down at her dark-eyed boy. "Who ever would have guessed?"

By the time she met Massimo at the airport the next day, she was breathless with suspicion. Still, her first reaction to catching sight of him, as always, was wonder that this man, lithe, elegant and a magnet of female glances, was her husband. "Mine," she thought, and then, "not another new suit?" Uncharacteristically, he had brought her a present, a gold chain necklace so heavy and thick that it looked fake.

"Next month , you and Alex must come with me."

Margaret was only becoming more convinced. "What are you transporting for the man? Drugs?" She did keep her voice light.

"You watch too much T.V. You have ever since Alex was born."

"How would you know what I watch or don't watch? You're always leaving me alone." She wanted to say much more but recriminations were not the way. She asked again.

She cajoled. She pleaded. It was only when she relived their welcoming hug that she found the key. "This new suit of yours . . ."

He talked after she threatened the jacket with scissors. It was money, only money. She should know how ridiculous Italy was about taking currency out of the country. After all, how could it be serious when Malvio had his own bank in the Bahamas?

It seemed to Margaret that she had taken frivolous risks rather than face the necessary one. On a long distance call, she told her mother so, but Jean misunderstood her and said, "You're getting a divorce." She was distressed but distracted by her own upcoming marriage.

"No. Yes, I am but that's not the risk I mean."

"The spark's gone."

"No, it's not that," she said remembering how she felt the last time he held her. "I can't be the wife he wants."

"Your father said something of the sort to me once. I held on."

"Massimo doesn't have your . . . flexibility or your patience."

"I'm not sure that I like your tone."

"It's not directed at you, Mother. Really."

Margaret and Massimo had been separated for five months, and he was in Venice with his ailing father when Lo Schiavo was found dead in his office, shot five times at point range. The murder, never solved, impelled Massimo in a way her words and tears had not. He quit his job and could not find a new one, not one worthy of him. Nearly each time he saw her, when picking up or dropping off Alex, he reminded her that it was her fault that he was in Canada and, therefore, alone and unemployed.

Margaret felt guilty that at such a time of financial difficulty she avoided any possible jobs. Her private exercises in watercolour had propelled her into more open experiments with acrylics, the paint trowelled on or squeezed straight from the tube, layers on layers, ever thicker. Then she had begun adding to the canvas: pieces of newspaper, bark, sand, slivers of bamboo. Her search for more texture, more presence, more satisfaction with what she made had become pressing. She couldn't waste her energy on a nine to five job. She was selling the odd painting, appearing and drawing praise in group shows. Then she changed direction again.

This time, yes, this time, she found her materials: rocks (jade and quartz, porphyry and diorite) wood, clay, feathers and paint. And she found the form to express what she had learned to see, gazing inwards and outwards. Why hadn't she figured it out before? Masks. Of course. In Venice, in the catalogue of her first show, *Mascara 1*, she was quoted as saying, "I found the way in a Canadian museum. Before a Cree Horse mask. It had a lightening, almost Picassolike design on a sky blue background..." She told the owners of the tiny gallery off Whyte Avenue that exhibited *Mascara II* that she'd been inspired by the traditional masks of the *carnivale*. "A placing aside, a transformation of the self. That's why the painted eyes above the eye holes. It's seeing both ways – double vision." Much later when interviewed by the Italian art magazine *Guardia*, she spoke of native traditions, ritual objects, protective talismans, mystical instruments.

Just after *Mascara II* opened, a gigantic bank scandal of international proportions broke in Italy. Malvio was arrested in Rio and a few months later took or, more likely, was given poison. Then while in Venice visiting his dying mother, Massimo finally found work with a design company that belonged to the Aga Khan.

Alex would learn to travel: back and forth, back and forth.

"I've always loved Italy," Maggie would say encouragingly as once more she pulled out his suitcase. Often she was able to accompany him. Her audience was more receptive and her work brought higher prices in Italy. "And you Alex," she would say, "are a legitimate heir."

HOME AND AWAY

Torino, September 10, 1986.

Cara Mamma e caro Papa,

Stop worrying! I'm fine, I'm great, I'm more than great.

And I know I made the right decision leaving the *nonni* and Roccagloriosa. I enjoyed my week there – really – but a week was enough. I went to the beach. I walked in the hills. I visited all your old stomping grounds like I knew you'd want me to: the café in the piazza, the dance pavilion by the sea, Zio Antonio's farm, where Dad proposed, San Giovanni where you were married. All your stories came back to me, and now, because I know the context, because I can mentally see where everything happened, they mean a lot more to me.

On the phone, both of you kept asking what was wrong. I repeat everyone was wonderful. That was part of the problem. I was fussed over from morning to night. And I thought you were bad! Every moment of the day was planned. I was escorted from house to house, meal to meal. "You must try this." "You must never drink cold drinks in this kind of heat." "I've been cooking all day, just a few bites." I felt like one of those force-fed geese, bound and fat. I said before I left that I wanted to find Italy, find the place I'd come from. If I stayed in Roccagloriosa, I would have come back to Edmonton remembering Italy as a series of rooms and meals.

What was the reaction when we left for Canada? Did everyone act as if it were a big tragedy? Years ago, Nonna told me, when people emigrated, their departure was marked by funeral rites. When they left the village, they ceased to exist.

Maybe that explains what I felt was a lack of interest in what kind of life you have made for yourselves in Canada. No one, not even the *nonni* or Zio Dario has asked about how it is for us. Oh, one cousin had seen a documentary on Canadian Natives and questioned me about racism and oppression. And both Nonna and Zia Fulvia were overjoyed when they found out their favourite soap opera (and yours, Mother) was three years behind, and I could foretell the future of Ashley and Hilary and Josh. But no one seems curious about our adopted home.

Gelsomina's regular boarder, a student, returns soon. I'm madly looking for a room and for a job. Tell Dodo I'll write soon.

Hugs, Anna.

Torino, September 16,1986.

Dear Dodo,

Thanks for trying to keep the parents calm and rational – no easy task. Especially since they've figured out, this is not a visit. I intend to stay. I can't face coming back to another year of clerking at Gladrags. On the phone, Mom sounded as if she were going to cry. "What, where, when, how, why, why, why..." Then it slipped out – that too familiar question. "Why can't you be more like your sister?" This time she meant why can't you march straight from school to college? Why can't you pick out a career, settle on a future? Achieve *like Dodo does.* Sigh.

I'm still looking for a room of my own. It's so difficult. I think there's a less than zero vacancy rate, with a waiting list for apartments. Gelsomina introduced me to Paola, a girl from Roccagloriosa. Tell the parents that she's the granddaughter of Mum's cousin Luigi. She works in a leather goods boutique and thinks she might eventually be able to get me in. They need girls with good English to wait on tourists. "But like this," she said, motioning to my hair, fingering the material of my sleeve, "you won't do." She meant that I need to look, as the girls here do, as if I stepped out of the latest *Elle* magazine. At first, I was really impressed by the elegance, but gradually I got bored with the uniformity. You know what it's like in Edmonton, everything goes from tacky to torn to designer togs. Here every woman over twenty-five wears a navy wool skirt and a coordinated blouse (though both are of better quality than you ever see at home.) The under twenty-five's sport tight capri polka-dotted pants. I tried resisting Paola for a day or so, but I gave in. I conformed to the fashion orthodoxy. I bought a pair.

I also have to work on my Italian. The problem is not my Canadian accent – that is considered charming, even chic. Paola says all the "in" people in Torino speak with a slight French or English intonation. What has to go is my tendency to speak in Mum and Dad's Neapolitan dialect. Even a trace of a Southern Italian accent connects you to all the workers who keep the Fiat going, the hordes in the cement block suburbs with loud voices and crime connections. *Terroni*, they call us, earth people, Arabs, Africans, implying, of course, that there is something wrong with being any of them.

Why Torino? I can hear you asking. Why the cold, closed North where you're a double stranger? Is there? Yes. There is. Harry Paderon from Edmonton is here playing hockey, which should explain everything for you but probably doesn't. I'm sure last year I told you some of what I felt for Harry but I don't think you were listening. (I hope you don't use your vague, condescending smile with your Grade Fours. They won't like it , believe me.) Don't mention this to the parents. As soon as they find out he's here, they'll panic.

Once when I was at the Paderons' for a sleepover with

Genni and Dad came over to bring my bag, he found me and Harry alone watching a hockey game. He grabbed my elbow and asked in a dramatic voice – what is going on here? Luckily, Harry was so involved in the game and his beer that he barely turned his head, and Genni arrived back from the store before Dad could drag me out. It was typical: Dad thinking the *worst* (I only wish), me embarrassed, Genni giggling, Harry oblivious.

Harry was too preoccupied to notice most things right then. All his life, since he was six years old, had been hockey and more hockey. "I was always brought along," he says. Always watched, always encouraged. And that reinforced his feeling that he was meant to play, as the song says, in the big league, that he was fated.

And it all happened for him – from PeeWees to Juniors to being drafted by the Oilers. But then, in his second game with the team, he dislocated his left shoulder. And he went back too soon and really wrecked it. A few minutes of ice time and he was shut out for the season and maybe for good. There were other teams, and there was always the minors, but he didn't feel that. Day after day, he sat at home, drinking beer and watching T.V. Unless there was a game on, he changed channels continually: click, click, pause, click.

I'd always liked him, but seeing him so often . . . well, it became something more. I asked you, keeping it all very abstract, how to get a man's attention. Remember? You said, "Either you have it or you don't." I didn't listen. I hung around in my cutest outfits, offering to get him videos, games, snacks. He'd smile and thank me, but kept his attention to himself.

Finally, this agent contacted him about playing for Torino. His shoulder was healing, and he started to see that another style of play, another kind of season might be possible. He also started to see me, in both senses. I'm sure you remember that, at least, the way I went on and on about it. What I didn't tell you, because I thought you would disapprove – don't be a chump, you'd say – was how panicky I felt at his leaving. I started to fantasize about me and him in Italy, away from Mum and Dad's curfews and questions. A different light, an Italian light, could make me look even more appealing.

He arrives back from training camp tomorrow.

I'm trusting you to keep quiet. Not a word.

Love, Ann.

Torino, Oct. 17.

Dear Genni,

I've done it. I'm here, settled with a room and a job. The room is large, high-ceilinged and close to the city centre. I have to share the bathroom and the kitchen, but my co-habitors (we are not mates, on any level) are rarely around. The two Ethiopian students creep in late and leave early. I suspect illegal jobs rather than dedication to study. The third co-habitor is a washed out platinum blonde, who works at night and sleeps all day. She leaves wearing full tart regalia and carrying a cellular phone. My job is at a store called *Prada*, which sells an exclusive line of leather goods, like Gucci, but snobbier. Paola, my friend who got me in, says that the Gladrags rules of smiles and service are not enough. I have to make each customer feel that I appreciate her exquisite taste. Only she has the sensitivity to choose that particular thousand dollar bag.

Paola arranged a makeover for me. Your brother Harry seems to think I'm "looking good." When I heard that he'd arrived back from training camp in the Dolomites, I went to the apartment building he's staying at, got the concierge to let me go up and rang his doorbell. Was he surprised! He stood at the door with his mouth open. Then he hugged me like I was the Stanley Cup.

I know he's not one for letters, so I thought I should fill you in on how well everything's going for Harry. Naturally playing for the Toros is not like playing for the Oilers. There's no sense of being at the centre of things, the division banners overhead, the monitors blinking, the organ pumping the fans and players up. The rinks are smaller, seating about 5,000, and often open air. Last week we were in one made of cedar, encircled by the Dolomites, quite breathtaking. And the fans are very keen and know the game surprisingly well.

Mr. Cecchetti, who owns the team, has put Harry in one of his penthouses with a terrace and a view. They expect him to eat every meal out, and all of his restaurant bills are covered. Harry told Mr.C. that he could cook for himself. Mr. C. just stared at him in disbelief. "But no," he said, "How could you?" As if, for a man, cooking – even breakfast – was as impossible as a woman playing in the National Hockey League. Harry's treated like a star. He says the Italian players watch everything he does. They imitate everything from the way he tapes his stick to how he laces up his skates. The fans hang around after the game to see him, to get his autograph. And the groupies! One in particular makes me sick. She looks and acts like she stepped out of a rock video (fawn, wiggle, quiver.) *"Dai, Arrigo,"* she says in this caramel candy voice.

The down side is that he's expected to be a star. He's like the American quarterbacks on our football teams, imported dazzle, and he's expected to score. He worked very hard at training camp. He was out of shape when he arrived and afraid they wouldn't keep him. He was pleased with his first game. He got two assists and hit a couple of guys. But in the dressing room, the coach told him if he kept up "the violence," he was out. Goals, the coach kept saying, think only of goals.

So Harry's adjusting to this style of play, to the emphasis on skating and clever moves. I'm adjusting to working and a surprising amount of partying. The game this Saturday is in Milan. Afterwards we're going down to the Riviera to a villa that belongs to an uncle of Mario (Harry's roommate.)

This is the life!

Love, Ann.

Torino, November 21.

Dear Dodo,

I'm glad the parents are less hysterical. I think it's a bit easier for them, because I'm in Italy and not New York or Toronto.

How are things going for you and this Allan you mentioned? He does sound like your type – serious. (The fact that you met at a how-to talk on composting says it all.) I wouldn't worry about his other "responsibilities," not if things feel right between you. Listen to my advice for a change. After all, how many years have I listened to yours?

Harry explained this process called *visualization* that athletes use to improve their performance. During practise, he might try a play over and over again, receiving the puck, say, shooting it on net. Then, before the game, he gathers all his concentration and mentally goes through the play.

He pictures himself scoring. That way, at the right time, his body and mind work together. The puck goes in. (Of course, there's always the goaltender or other players to mess things up.) So what am I trying to say? Get your body in shape. Visualize you and Allan together. Mentally practise your moves. Concentrate, and the relationship can be yours. Back when Harry barely said hello, I started imagining us talking, our bodies drawing closer, closer, until the magic moment. Every ounce of me imagined our lips, our inner selves, meeting. I wanted it so much that it had to happen. And it did. It has. Almost daily.

I'm sending you these pictures one of his friends took, so you can see for yourself. Pass them on to the parents, except for the one with his head buried in my neck. My favourite is the shot where he's holding me upside down. You can see how much we've been giggling.

Last night we went out to dinner, just the two of us. We talked till late, and walking back home, he bought me a rose from a gypsy child who was standing out in the cold of a piazza, accosting all who passed. I started to cry. I was both sad for the child who'd had to learn to hustle so young and happy my hustle had worked. And Harry put his hand to my face and said, "That's what I've always loved about you – you're sensitive."

Today we went out shopping with Paola. Harry was used to wearing a suit and tie to the games, but when he got here he was told that it wasn't necessary, that he should feel free to express the real him. Harry started wearing his sweats. Until he noticed that the inner self being expressed was supposed to be elegant and fashionable. Now we both have new, pricey wardrobes.

Actually, many things here are not how I expected them to be. Remember how we used to make fun of Mum and the way she would dismiss whatever we were pleading for: a perm, snug jeans, a sleepover, all with "Ok for these Canadians. We're Italians." Anyway, between her rules and Dad's angry comments about the looseness of Canadian morals, I really thought that here everyone went to church and girls were still chaperoned on dates. Hah! Instead I found topless beaches, porno movies on T.V. and lascivious pictures of naked women on the cover of not *Playboy*, but serious magazines, the equivalent of our *Maclean's* or *Saturday Night*. And if you saw the way these groupies act . . . I asked Mario how he would classify them. He assured me they were respectable girls, students from good families.

Which reminds me, I've got to know the blonde in the next room. Zaira stopped me in the hall and asked if I would translate the lyrics of Madonna's "Like a Virgin," for her.

Remember, visualize!

Your cheerful sister.

Torino, Jan. 22.

Dear Dodo,

Why does it take you so long to answer? I wait and wait for your reaction. And when your letter does finally arrive you are talking of things that happened months ago! Writing letters home feels like that game we used to play at school, the one where you whispered a message in the ear of the person next to you, who passed it on to the next who, in turn, passed it on. By the end of the line, the message was completely changed. The Italian and Canadian postal systems are the worst in the world and sending a letter through both takes forever. Do you know I've never actually found out what postage is necessary to send a letter from here to there? Each time I ask I get a different answer. I thought the clerks were trying to cheat me because I'm a foreigner, but Paola assured me the clerks don't know what the postage is. They have to guess.

I've been going through a bad stretch. I've been home from work a week with the flu. And it's hard to get better with my room so cold and damp. I'm in bed right now fully dressed, several layers and I'm still cold. I haven't talked to Harry in two weeks. There was this party at the penthouse. I was out on the terrace with Mario. It was a crisp, clear evening, and the cigarette smoke inside was making my nose run. He was asking me what I thought of Bruce Cockburn, who he'd seen twice in concert. Before I could answer one of the defencemen on the team butted in. "You like Whitney Houston? I love Whitney Houston. What means, "You give good love." Then, switching into Italian, "Would you translate this song for me?" He was standing too close, breathing on me.

I turned away. And then I saw through the glass door. That groupie/slut I've mentioned before was standing right up against Harry. I saw her lay her hand on the back of his neck. I stood in the dark, with the other two yammering, and I watched them kiss. You can imagine. I'd been outplayed, finessed, a Tic Tac Toe move. I didn't sleep much that night; I kept watching the replay: her hand on his neck, his bending towards her . . . But then I convinced myself I shouldn't have run off. (I got Mario to drive me home.) I called him before breakfast. I knew I shouldn't, but I couldn't stop myself. I had to hear his voice and his reassurrances. As soon as he answered, I knew she was with him, lying there with him. "You disappeared suddenly," he said. "I'm tied up all day," he said.

I keep telling myself: it's not over, till it's over. I can rally, turn on the offense. An unexpected play and . . . But I also keep asking myself why was it so easy for her (to score)? Where was Harry's defence?

Phone me if you can.

Red-eyed and nosed, Anna.

Torino, Feb. 5.

Dear Dodo,

I just received the letter you wrote on Dec. 11 where you tell me that you're happy to know that I'm so happy, but where you warn me to be careful, to take it slow (as you are with Allan.) Too late, sis. But you'll have figured that out before you read this.

Until last night, I avoided Harry. Then Mario insisted I go with him to a team dinner, and I thought seeing Harry again might help me decide what to do. He wasn't with the slut, not for most of the evening. He sat down beside me. I moved to a chair across and down the table. He shouted over the music and the space. "How are you?" "I worry about you." Many of the players and their girls were listening, watching. He called me *carissima*, dearest one. I felt as if I were looking at him through glass, as if that terrace door was permanently between us, shutting him off from me.

At the fruit and cheese course, *she* made an entrance, sliding into place beside him. I continued to chew and swallow. But I couldn't taste what was on my tongue. I couldn't smell either the wine or the food. Mario was joking, trying to distract me. I had to watch his lips to catch what he said.

Sunday, when, as usual, I fixed Canadian breakfast for Paola and Zaira, fried eggs, *pancetta*, and toast, Zaira began to lecture me. "All men are jerks," she said, dipping bread into yolk. "Now you know. There are a lot worse than him, believe me. So he's puffed up like a balloon from the attention. Floating here and there. It won't last."

I tried to tell them how important Harry had been for me, how all I'd ever wanted was to be close to him. It was the only thing I'd ever been sure of, and now I wasn't sure. Not at all.

"Zaira's right," Paola said. "Her appeal will wane; she's exotic for him, a taste of Italy. You are Canada. And he will come home."

But will I wait for him? When I try to explain things to you, I start to understand them myself. And, as I wrote down my friends' words, I could suddenly feel how much I've lost.

I was wrong about who Harry was. And I was wrong to think that if we came back to this country where we were born, we could both discover ourselves and each other. When Harry walks into his local bar every morning for a cappuccino, he's greeted with "*Ehi, Americano.*" I blend in visually and verbally, but everyone sees I'm a foreigner from the way I move, walk, hold myself. To Harry I am the familiar, good old Anna. To the men here, like Mario, I'm the exotic, the girl from the land of ice and snow.

I'll be back by spring.

Anna.

Edmonton, March 21.

Dear Harry,

I'm sitting at the desk in my room, happy to be home, happy to be surrounded again by the – Harry.

Think what you want. I did not run away. I left because it was the right time for *me* to leave –

Dear Harry,

You're right. My parents are thrilled –

Edmonton, March 21.

Dear Harry,

I am not surprised that you decided to re-sign with the Toros for next year. I'm sure the deal was enticing. Italians believe in paying for quality. Still, it does seem odd to think of you wearing the Italian colours, playing for the national team. By now you must realize that you aren't quite Italian. Though, of course, since fourteen of the sixteen players are Italian-Canadian, you will fit right in. And the World Championships will be exciting, a learning process.

That's what Torino was for me. I came back and applied to the university. I'm interested in Anthropology.
Thanks for the letter. I know you hate to write.
I'll see you when you get home.
Love, Anna.

On a Platter

Fulvia was not one for waxing nostalgic. "I'm not the type," she told Anne. "You know that about me by now." Which was why it was so startling to find herself caught – in the middle of their ladies lunch at The Happy Gardens, in the middle of Moo Shui pork and pancakes and tea – caught and locked in memory, as the words "this takes me back . . ." slipped from her mouth. And she paused. She apologized. "Not me," she told Anne.

She hated it when Nino launched, as he did too often, into a paean of the glories of Italian ice cream or coffee, mothers or cheese graters: Italian anything when he was in his remember/ remember mood. "Sure," she'd say. "Tell me another one." Or, borrowing one of their daughter Barbara's phrases, "Give me a break." "Your memory's faulty," she'd begin, marshalling facts to puncture and deflate his nostalgia balloon.

Fulvia was not one even for remembering. Her childhood was closed off, walled up, thousands of miles and twenty years away. Barbara was so used to listening to her father – the tale of the cowpattie, the fall into the lagoon, an entire volume of legends – that lately she was asking for her mother's stories. And each time Fulvia was stuck; she could call up no equivalent. And what she could have called up – what she knew lurked behind those stone walls topped with broken glass – couldn't be spoken of. Couldn't, shouldn't. Just the thought of remembering made a jagged shard twist in her chest.

"They can't be all bad," Barbara said. "Don't you remember anything happy?"

"I must have forgotten," Fulvia said. "But have I told you about how your father and I met? Or about the time you smeared diaper cream all over your furniture? Never mind the long ago and far away."

Never mind. Fulvia's memories tended to be rare and involuntary, physiological responses beyond her control. (Never *from* the mind, never *in* the mind. Or not for long.) Sensations rather than scenes. Sensations of sun, light, heat, dark, enclosure, shame that she associated with her childhood, with Sicily.

Long ago and far away. I am lucky, Fulvia thought. I see nothing, I meet no one to remind me. Nino's crazy to want to move back. Just look at Anne, who'd been born and spent nearly all her years in Edmonton; it seemed as if whenever they were out together they ran into someone from her past. They had barely sat down at their table when a bearded man, Eddie Bauer Parka and moon boots, stopped on his way to the door. "Anne, longtime . . ." he'd said. From his smile and Anne's, Fulvia presumed he was another old boyfriend. He was introduced as "a friend from way back." Let the back stay back and the past, past, Fulvia thought. Nino must have known she wouldn't agree to go back. Why was he so insistent? So self-righteous?

For better or for worse, he reminded her, only slightly tongue in cheek, you swore. And she had sworn, dressed in white lace with orange flower blossoms in her hair, she had sworn, but here in a clean, bare Canadian church, and not there, not encased in the baroque excess of St. Agatha's.

Here. The restaurant was cheery with year-round Christmas decorations, shiny balls and silvery garlands, noisy with patrons flushed by the February snow and ice outside and the steamy warmth inside. Anne and Fulvia's table was squeezed into the middle of a throughway. Waitresses, arms laden with plates, bustled by.

Anne and Fulvia had been having lunch together for years, from the time they both worked at a dress shop. Since then their lives had gone in different directions: Fulvia had been at home with the infant Barbara during the years when Anne had been most career-driven, now Fulvia had her boutique, and Anne was tied down by three year old twins. Still, despite their differences, which were not just situational, their friendship survived. Mostly because of Anne, it survived: she was the one who cultivated and tended, the one who phoned.

And Fulvia was almost always happy to hear from her. Though there had been a stretch early on, after Anne had been a dental hygienist for a year, when Anne's view of humanity had become so dark – "People lie," she would repeat over and over again, "you can't trust anyone" – that Fulvia had avoided her. Luckily, Anne had come to understand what her job was doing to her. She returned to university, saving herself from permanent pessimism and those around her from conversational ennui.

Now Anne and Fulvia talked about all sorts of things: the minutiae of their lives, motherhood, bargains, weight loss, whatever issue was flavour of the month. Today, since Fulvia had been called in by her gynecologist because (as he explained it) "there's a spot on your mammograms that falls into the grey area," they were exchanging medical stories. "I asked her to check my thyroid," Anne was saying, " but she kept insisting I was suffering from depression."

"You should have filed a complaint," Fulvia said. "I would have."

"I have no doubt about that ... Try these, Fulvia. They're delicious." The platters of food exhaled foreign and comforting smells: ginger and soy and lemongrass. And when Fulvia took a bite, the flavours were distinct, sharp and salty.

"I don't trust doctors," Fulvia said.

Anne smiled affectionately. "You don't trust – period."

"Don't let Nino hear you. He's always looking for ammunition."

"He accuses you . . . ?" Anne said.

"Of all kinds of things when he's in that mood." Fulvia noticed that Anne's blue eyes, behind her gold-rimmed glasses, were alert, focussed. Anne loved any kind of emotional revelation. "How do you *really* feel about that?" was one of her habitual questions.

"This sounds serious."

"Not at all," Fulvia said, keeping her voice light. "Well, he's always had his moods. We've discussed that before."

"But this is something different? Something worse?"

"It's this recession. He insists the company's on the edge of bankruptcy."

"Oh no."

"I went over the books. And it isn't in danger. Not really. A few changes. That's all that's needed."

"You've always had such a good head for business. He should let you run things. He must realize that."

"Umm. Give up the boutique for construction? I don't think so."

"Of course not – just help him out a bit."

"Let's have dessert," Fulvia said. "I feel like stuffing myself today. They must have something disgustingly sweet."

"I crave sugar when I'm tense too," Anne said. "Are you *very* upset about the mammograms? . . . Well, of course, you are. Who wouldn't be? You can sit there, as impassive as ever . . . but inside . . ."

Fulvia lifted one shoulder in the smallest of shrugs. "I'm

going to get a second opinion. Probably a third. Before and, if necessary, after the biopsy. So I can chose the best course of action."

Fulvia had intended to stay calm with Nino, to discuss things rationally. Instead, faced with his intransigence, she had found herself shouting. 'You don't make a decision about moving back and then expect me to go along with it. You don't choose for me. No one does."

For better or for worse, he had said. Here or there.

Gently, insidiously, last night's dream came back to her, like a dropped white-gauze curtain, separating her from the bustle of the restaurant. She was alone in church, her old church, white marble carved into a confusion, a riot, a jungle of leaves, garlands, cherubs, saints: the plenty of earth and heaven. St. Agatha's, gold daubed statues, a glowing, gory painting, a wall of hand-written pleas and testimonials, blurred snapshots and silver amulets, hundreds of them: hands, arms, legs, eyes. Currying favour. But not her. She was alone. Before the altar. And she would not bend her head. She refused, and her refusal was hard and sharp against the shifting sickness set off by that unchecked excess.

A dream? A memory? She struggled to push away the gauze curtain and focus clearly on Anne and the platters of food. That was there and then, she reassured herself. Long ago and far away. For not just a few years and thousands of miles lay between Alcamo and Edmonton. The gap was one of centuries. It could not be bridged. Time was not reversible. Nino was wrong headed. No plane could take them back. It was impossible.

"Earth to Fulvia, come on, try one," Anne was saying. "You insisted on ordering these. You haven't been listening, have you? Don't apologize. I'd be in a worse state than you. I remember when I got a positive pap smear. It turned out to be nothing- a yeast infection, but for three months..."

It was then that it happened. Fulvia bit into the bun and the sweet, elusive flavour teasing her tongue caught her (was there no escape today) caught her and she remembered – Sicily. Though it took a moment before she actually identified the taste, before she understood what had been recalled. "This takes me back," she found herself saying. "*Zuccata*, these preserves the cook used to make. Boiled summer squash and jasmine water. Heavenly." She paused.

"The cook?" Anne said. "I never imagined you with a cook. It's not my image of you at all."

"We rarely made desserts at home. They were bought. Mostly from the local convent. Only on special occasions, thank goodness. You can't imagine, Anne, how amazing, how subtle they were. The triumph of gluttony they've been called. Those nuns must have poured all their blocked sensual appetites into their culinary creations. *Minni di virgini*, the base was a pastry crust of almond flour, then layers of *zuccata* alternating with sponge cake and custard, topped with almond paste, and on top of the mound – you see they're called Virgin's breasts – a red cherry."

"You got these from the convent?"

"They're named for St. Agatha, a much beloved Sicilian saint, to commemorate her mutilation and martyrdom. Each convent had their own version, their own triumph. Sicilian sweets are the best in the world. Nothing comes close." Fulvia pushed away the dish with the remains of the bun. "I'm sorry."

"Why? It's fascinating."

"Ah yes, you told me you started in anthropology . . . ritual foods among the primitives."

Anne looked startled, perhaps even hurt. "Don't be silly. Honestly, Fulvia, sometimes..."

"I am sorry. I just caught myself off-guard. I hate that. All this remembrance of things past – I'm not the type. You know that about me by now."

"What's the harm? It does one good. And lets your friends understand who you are. I mean, I had this view of your childhood which I now see was all wrong."

"Ah, the cook."

"Was it just her? Did you have other servants?"

"Inside and out."

"Your family had money then."

"No end to it."

"And you..."

"I withstood temptation. I got out. I left it behind. " Did Anne guess? Her cheeks and eyes were glowing with curiosity. 'What's the harm?' she'd said. And, of course, it was the fashion, using one's past, like decolleté or a miniskirt: look at me, pay attention, childhood trauma as titillating accessory, a spike heel shoe or a white lace bustier. "It wasn't easy." Fulvia could go no farther. She could not brush away the jagged shards. She could never knock down the wall. If she tried to flaunt those stones, if she fashioned them into a folkloristic necklace, they would break her neck or, worse, her daughter's neck, so long and straight and slender.

Nino had let himself be tempted. He wanted to go back. "I'm free here," she said to him for the thousandth time. "There I'd be shut in. Trapped."

"You only think of yourself," Nino repeated yet again. "For me, it's a way out."

Fulvia waved to the waiter for the bill. "Look at the time. I'll be late for the appointment if I don't get moving."

Anne nodded. "This has been good. Let's not wait so long next time. We could go out to dinner. Have more time to talk."

"I'll have to see," Fulvia said, buttoning up her coat. "I'm not sure." She pushed open the inner door and then the iced outer one. Anne was right behind her, still chatting. Fulvia took a deep breath of the cold, clean air.

"Next week," Anne was saying, "I have to finish that presentation but by, say, Friday . . ."

Fulvia pulled back her coat sleeve to check her watch. As she noted the time, she saw the date: February 9. The feast of Saint Agatha. So that was it. There was nothing sinister, nothing psychic about her sudden memories.

"You're a hard woman," Nino had said. "You only think of yourself. You don't consider me. Always. Part of you has always been beyond reach, untouchable."

"Don't put *me* in the wrong. What's right is right."

"See, little-Miss-Purity. This is the real world, Fulvia. Not black, not white: grey."

All these years of marriage and he still didn't understand. It was not grey; it was either/ or. And she had chosen here, she had chosen white. (Lace, jasmine, snow.)

"Call me as soon as you get the results of the biopsy," Anne said, as they stood by Fulvia's Taurus. "I'm sure it will be all right."

Suddenly Fulvia was afraid. She saw again the murky painting in her old church, the painting of St. Agatha carrying the platter with her sacrificial breasts. She saw the wall of offerings, the riot of metal amulets. She was not inviolable. And she knew too well what would be required of her.

MEMBER OF THE SCABRINI GROUP
Quebec, Canada
2000